THE CHALET
SCHOOL AND
THE LINTONS

ELINOR M. BRENT-DYER

Armada

Dedicated to Kathleen and Vera Park with love and very many
thanks from Elinor

First published by W. & R. Chambers Ltd.,
London and Edinburgh.
First published in this revised Armada edition in 1973 by
Fontana Paperbacks,
8 Grafton Street, London W1.

This impression 1983

© W. & R. Chambers

Printed in Great Britain by
William Collins Sons & Co. Ltd, Glasgow

CHAPTER I

THE DOCTOR'S VERDICT

THERE was a silence in the consulting-room. The great physician sat back in his chair, and sighed softly to himself. No doctor likes to give an unfavourable verdict, and he was no exception to the rule. The pale-faced woman in the chair opposite him sat thinking hard.

"Then you think, Doctor," she said at length, "that if I do as you suggest there may be—a chance?"

"Certainly I do, Mrs. Linton. I wish you had come to me sooner, for then it would have been easier. As it is, I consider that if you will do as I have said, it is more than probable that you will be cured finally, even though it may take a long time. You have let things go very far, but if you will go to the Sanatorium at the Sonnalpe, and put yourself completely into the hands of the doctors there, I think you have a very good chance indeed of recovery."

Mrs. Linton nodded. She had the air of only half-listening to what he was saying, and he wondered what was passing through her mind.

Suddenly she looked up. "You see, Doctor, I have more than myself to consider. I told you I am a widow. But I have two girls—Gillian is fifteen, and Joyce is fourteen. We have no relations in England to whom I could send them while I am away, so if I go, it means boarding-school."

The doctor nodded thoughtfully. "I see!" He got up, and took a turn or two up and down the room. Then he came to his desk again, and began hunting among the papers there, even while his patient was fastening her coat. He found what he wanted, and sat down again. "Don't go yet, Mrs. Linton. I rather think I may be able to help you." He glanced at his tablet. "Ah! I see you are the last patient this afternoon. That is good. Now I am going to ask you one or two questions. You say you have no one to whom you could entrust the girls?"

"No one," said Mrs. Linton with quiet decision.

"I see. Well, I wonder if you have ever heard that on the Tiernsee, the lake which lies at the foot of the Sonnalpe group, there is an excellent school for girls? One, moreover, that is run on English lines."

She shook her head. "No; I never heard of it. Indeed, I had never heard of the Sonnalpe till this afternoon."

"Well, the school is there. My friend, Dr. Russell, the head of the Sanatorium, married the head-mistress of it —she is a very charming woman, too—nearly three years ago. Mrs. Russell has had to give up her work, of course; but she still retains a financial interest in it, and is also very much interested in the work. Her partner, Mademoiselle Lepâttre, is an excellent teacher; the school is very well staffed, and there is a large number of girls. The daughter of another friend of mine, Rosalie Dene, was there till she was seventeen, and was very happy. Mrs. Russell's own young sister, Joey Bettany, is head-girl now, I believe."

"Rosalie Dene? Is she the daughter of Canon Dene of St. Aloysius' in Bakerfield?" asked Mrs. Linton. "I know them slightly. I have met Rosalie with Mrs. Dene, and thought she seemed a charming girl."

"Yes; you are quite right there. This school began with very small numbers, I believe. But it has grown and prospered. The Sanatorium has, of course, added to its numbers. Many of the girls there have parents undergoing treatment at the Sonnalpe, and the doctors at the Sonnalpe keep a watchful eye on them always. Lately, they opened an annexe up on the alpe for specially delicate children. Do you know Charles Stevens, the author of *Glorious Prague*? His younger child is at the annexe, though I believe the elder girl is at the school itself. And

6

Professor Benson—the great authority on Aeschylus—he died about a year ago, you may remember—his only child is there too. Now could you not send your girls to the Chalet School? I think you told me that you were fairly well off? The fees are not so very heavy. And there is this to be said for it that could not be said of any English school: it is directly under the eye of doctors who watch over the girls, and look for any symptoms of trouble, so that they may be checked at once. Girls like yours are particularly guarded, and the whole régime has been drawn up with an eye to strengthening the girls. Then again, should you want them at any time, they will be within easy distance of you. Besides, I expect they will be allowed to spend occasional weekends at the Sonnalpe to see you."

Mrs. Linton looked at him with hope dawning in her eyes. His verdict—that she was suffering from the tuberculosis that is the white man's scourge—had been a terrible shock to her. His pronouncement that her only chance of life was to go to this Sanatorium had added to it. Her two girls were the dearest things in life to her, for her husband had died when Joyce, the younger girl, had been a baby of three. The thought of being separated from them like that, perhaps for months on end, had hurt her more than his verdict. But this sounded feasible.

"What about vacancies?" she asked. "It is November now—early December. They may have no room for next term; and you say that I ought to go at once——"

"Indeed you must," he said gently. "You ought not to remain in England a day longer than is necessary. If you will listen to me, you will put all yours affairs into the hands of your solicitor. He can close your house for you; or if you prefer it, he could place the furniture in storage, and let it—it is your own, I suppose?"

"Yes; it is my own," she said.

"Then if I may advise, do the latter. It will be at least three years before you should come back to England. It may even be more. But," he added, glancing out of the

7

window, "it is getting late, and the sun is setting. You ought not to be out now. So I must send you home. But here—here is the address. Write to-night, and when you have had a reply, come and see me again. We must get you out of England as quickly as possible. Now keep up your heart. I am sure they will be able to take your girls; and the men at the Sonnalpe will pull you through all right."

Mrs. Linton smiled faintly. "I feel as though it might be possible now. I can't thank you, Doctor, for your kindness, but I *am* grateful. And I will ring you up as soon as I hear from the school, and then you will tell me what we have to do."

"That is right. Have you a car?—No? Then my man will call a taxi for you. Remember; you must save yourself as much as possible. Now good-bye. I shall expect to see you next week."

With a final grip of the hand, he resigned her to his butler, bidding him summon a taxi; and then, regardless of the fact that it was tea-time, he turned to his desk once more, and called up the exchange, bidding them put him through to Innsbruck in the Tyrol as soon as possible. Then he ran upstairs to his wife's drawing-room where he enlisted her sympathy for the widow and her two girls, getting her to promise to help with any shopping for the children that might be necessary. Later, in the evening, he managed to get Dr. James Russell on the telephone, and had a brief and costly conversation with him.

Meanwhile, Mrs. Linton made her journey homewards to the pretty suburb, an hour out of London, where she had come to live when Gillian and Joyce had outgrown the little private school in the village in which they had formerly made their home. Now the two went to a big high school where Gillian was doing well at lessons, and Joyce was the most popular girl in her own set, though at work she did not shine, being lazy in the extreme. It was after five when she reached the pretty villa where they lived, and Gillian was on the look-out for her. As the gate-latch clicked, the girl ran to open the hall-door and let a flood of light on to the dark path.

"This is a nice time of day for a coldy person to be out!" she exclaimed in tones of mock severity. "Where-ever have you been, Mummy? Come along in to the fire at once!"

Mrs. Linton went in, the girl's strong young arm round her slight figure. She was tired out with her day in town and the shock the doctor had given her, and she panted slightly as she sank into the deep armchair which had been pulled up to the hearth. Joyce, who had been curled up on the rug, reading a school story and basking in the heat like a blissful salamander, scrambled to her feet, and went off to tell the maid to bring tea, while Gillian gently slipped off her mother's outdoor things, and brought her slippers.

"Don't talk yet, darling," she said anxiously. "You're rather breathless. Have you been hurrying? You shouldn't have done it."

Eva, the maid, brought in the dainty tray, and Gillian busied herself with pouring out tea, so the question was left unanswered. Mrs. Linton sipped her tea, and nibbled a wafer of bread-and-butter, and even managed to swallow some sponge-cake, though it was an effort. But with those keen dark-blue eyes on her, she dared do no less, and already Gillian was looking at her anxiously.

"You haven't eaten *anything*!" scolded the girl gently as her mother shook her head at the bread-and-butter. "Aren't you well, Mummy?"

"Just this horrid cough that won't go," said Mrs. Linton lightly. "Joyce, my pet, come here and tell me what you have been doing with yourself to-day. Did Miss Smythe excuse the Latin?"

"No—horrid pig!" said Joyce, as she dropped down at her mother's feet and laid her fair head against her. "I had to take a deten, and I didn't get home till nearly five. Mummy, *can't* I give up Latin? I do hate it so, and I'm not a bit of good at it."

9

Mrs. Linton laughed. "Little dunce!" she said, slipping a caressing hand over the silky golden waves against her knee. "No; of course you must go on with it! If you gave it up, you would have to take German instead, and I don't think you would like that any better," she added.

"I hate all lessons," grumbled Joyce. "I wish I didn't have to do any. It's all very well for Gill—she likes them!"

"Well, unless you are prepared to take German, I'm afraid you must go on with the Latin," said her mother, a trace of weariness in her tones.

Gillian noted it at once. "Joyce, get up!" she said peremptorily. "You make Mummy tired, lying against her like that."

Joyce laughed, and kept her place. "Mummy likes it," she said saucily. "You do, don't you, darling?"

Mrs. Linton shook her head at her. "Is all the prep done to-night, my lazy-bones? What about yours, Gill?"

"I've done everything but history," said Gillian. "Thursday is a free afternoon for me, you know."

"And my Joyce—what about you?"

"Oh, I'm too comfy to move," said Joyce lazily.

"I'm afraid you must, though. I can't write you any more notes this week. Besides, I have a letter to see to that must go off with the seven o'clock clearance. So run along to the dining-room, pet, and do your best.—Gill, bring my writing-case, dear. And perhaps you'll take the letter to the post afterwards."

Joyce got up reluctantly. "I don't see why you can't give me a note," she grumbled. "And why on earth is there such a rush about your letter?"

"It is business, and can't wait. Run along to your work, Baby."

Still grumbling, Joyce betook herself to the dining-room, where she gave her lessons a sketchy preparation which next day brought down on her head the wrath of four mistresses. Meanwhile, Mrs. Linton wrote her letter

10

to the address in the Tyrol which the doctor had given her, and then handed it to Gillian to post. The girl ran off, heedless of the change that very letter was to bring to them all, and when she came back, she sat down quietly with her history, while her mother rested in the big chair, half-dozing at times, and coughing every now and then the little hard cough which had forced her to pay that visit to the specialist.

The next few days passed as usual, except that Mrs. Linton quietly made what preparations she could for the move while the girls were at school. On the Saturday, there was trouble with Joyce, who wanted her mother to take them to the local cinema to see a big picture. Mrs. Linton was obliged to refuse, for all public assemblies had been forbidden her. Not yet could she bring herself to tell the girls what lay before them, so she could give no reason beyond her tiredness and cough, and Joyce sulked all the day over it. Then, just before bedtime, their mother had an attack of palpitation and breathlessness that alarmed poor Gillian horribly, and even made the younger girl ashamed of her bad behaviour. When it was over, poor Mrs. Linton felt obliged to tell the girls that she had seen a doctor, and he had forbidden any expeditions. But she felt that she could tell them nothing further until she had heard from the Tyrol.

Fortunately, the expected letter arrived by the midday post, for that talk of the great specialist's over the 'phone had resulted in an air-mail communication from the school, and Mrs. Linton learnt that all was well and her girls would be accepted in the school for the Easter term. Mademoiselle Lepâttre explained that though they would be in the same house for the first term, Joyce would be moved to the new chalet they were building for the younger Middles after Easter, while Gillian would stay in the original building. She also said that the girls would be allowed to spend week-ends up at the Sonnalpe, where they would stay with one or other of the married doctors, visiting their mother from there. Naturally, these visits

11

must be regulated by Mrs. Linton's own condition and the doctors' wishes, but she would be permitted to see as much of them as possible. The rest of the letter was taken up with inventories of what they would require, and ended with a request for a cabled reply, as the Chalet School had few vacancies, and they already had a waiting-list.

Mrs. Linton rang up her specialist, and telling him briefly what she had heard, made an appointment for that afternoon, and then went to lie down to recover herself a little. When she felt stronger, she wrapped up, and went out to send her cable. The next thing was to go to the High School, and she went after lunch, and explained matters to the head-mistress, who was very sympathetic, and agreed that the girls must go with their mother.

The next afternoon saw her in the consulting-room once more, and when the great physician had seen Mademoiselle's letter, he examined his patient thoroughly again.

"When do you start?" he asked when it was over.

"I suppose it must be as soon as possible, Doctor. I think I could manage next week, if that would suit."

He looked at her keenly. "It will suit the Sonnalpe people all right," he said. "But I hope you understand that you cannot take the journey at one stretch. It must be done very gradually, and will, I am afraid, occupy at least a week. I shall send a nurse with you, of course, and she will take complete charge of you all. You will stay or move on as she sees fit, and you must promise me to obey her implicitly. I want you to realise," he added gravely, "that I am still anxious to know that you are safely there. You will find it very fatiguing, I'm afraid, though Nurse Richards will do her best to make things easy for you. Don't permit your girls to make any demands on you at all. You need all your strength to get to the Sonnalpe."

"I'm sure they won't worry us, Doctor," said Mrs. Linton. "Joyce is only a baby, I know. But Gillian is a dear, good girl, and she will look after her sister. I will put myself right into Nurse's hands, and be as obedient

12

as possible," she added, with a little laugh that brought back the cough.

He frowned as he noted it, but said nothing. Instead, he left her, and presently came back with something to soothe it. When it was ended, and she was lying back in her chair, still panting, he spoke again. "You see what I mean. This cough wears you out. Now I am going to take you upstairs to my wife, who will give you some tea. Then, as I shall not need my car till late to-night, I am going to tell my chauffeur to drive you straight home, and you must go to bed and stay there till noon to-morrow. Please don't trouble about anything. If you have no near friend to see to it, my wife will be delighted to get the girls' clothes." Then he added a little shakily: "Our girl left us when she was only a few months old—and we never had another. She would have been just the age of your eldest if she had lived."

After that, Mrs. Linton felt that she could trust both him and his wife in anything, and after she had had her tea, she gladly consented to letting Lady Talbot take the girls to get their outfits. Then she was taken downstairs in the lift, and carefully put into the car, and the chauffeur received orders to drive slowly. He was very careful, but by the time she got home, she had realised the truth of the doctor's dictum that any journey would wear her out, and was thankful to go to bed.

The girls were late in coming home from school, as Gillian's form had given a tea-party to the rest of the Seniors and the Middles, so that it was after nine when they got in. They were met by Eva, who told them that their mother had gone to bed as she was tired, and begged that they would not go in that night, because she felt so worn out, and might be asleep.

"Goodness! That's not like Mummy!" said Joyce. "Are you sure she said that, Eva?"

"Certain, Miss Joyce.—I've got your suppers in the dining-room, Miss Gillian, and the cocoa's just ready. Cook was boiling it up when I came to answer the door.

13

The mistress looks tired to death, Miss Gill. She does indeed."

"Oh, all right, we won't disturb her," said Gillian, but she looked rather blank.

Joyce was soon asleep that night, and slept her usual sound, healthy slumbers. But Gillian lay awake for a very long time, and a cold dread of what was to come seemed to lie on her heart like a lump of ice.

CHAPTER II

GOOD-BYE TO ENGLAND!

"LEAVE the horrid old High School and go to a school abroad! Oh, Mummy, what a gorgeous idea! How topping of that ripping doctor to suggest it!"

This was Joyce, of course. Her volatile mind quite overlooked the fact that it was their mother's illness which had brought about the new state of affairs, and she was merely thrilled at the thought of quitting the High School, where she was always at feud with one or other of the mistresses, and going to a new school where her reputation for laziness was unknown. "Besides, in a foreign school they will give most of the time to dancing and manners and speaking French and things like that," she thought complacently.

But Gillian swung round on her for once. "Joyce, you are horrid!" Then she turned to her mother. "Mummy darling, what exactly does the doctor say about you? What's really wrong with you?"

Mrs. Linton hesitated a moment. "He says that I am not strong, and must go to the mountains for the sake of the air, and have this new treatment to help me throw off this stupid cold," she said finally. Not for worlds would she have alarmed her girls with the actual truth, and already Gillian was looking worried.

Joyce put on an injured expression. "How am I horrid, pray? I never have pretended to be mad over the old High. And Skinny has been beastly to me lately—all this term, in fact. She makes favourites, and it isn't fair."

"She doesn't scold the people who work decently, you mean," said Gillian. Then she was silent, for her mother had thrown her an appealing glance, as if asking her not to quarrel. Besides, she knew Joyce's calm insouciance by this time. So she gave it up, and listened with a certain amount of interest to the answers Mrs. Linton was giving to Joyce's questions.

"I have to be at this big hospital, you see, and it will take some time for the cure. I couldn't very well leave you two to look after yourselves in England; so when Dr. Talbot told me of this school, it struck me as being the very thing for you. It lies beside the Tiernsee, which is the lake at the foot of the mountain. And it doesn't take so very long to reach the Sonnalpe from it, for at the far end they have built a broad carriage-road; and in summer, you can climb up by a path near the lake. I wonder how you will like it? It means, for one thing, that you must speak French and German as well as your own language. Mademoiselle Lepâttre—"

"Who's she?" interrupted Joyce.

"She is the acting-Head of the School. The other Head is Mrs. Russell, wife of Dr. Russell at the Sonnalpe. But she doesn't teach now. When Mademoiselle wrote to me, she said that the girls learnt to speak all three languages, and you would have to learn them, too."

"Oh, well, I suppose we'll pick up a good deal by hearing the others," said Joyce lightly. "Go on, Mummy; tell us some more."

"Haven't you got the prospectus?" asked Gillian.

"Yes, dear. It's on my dressing-table. Will you run and fetch it?"

Gillian went off, and presently came back with the prospectus, and the three spent a happy hour turning it over and examining the photographs with which it was illustrated.

"I like their winter-sports kit," said Gillian. "It's so sensible; there's nothing to get in the way. But what *huge* boots! And isn't *that* a pretty girl!"

"Where? Let me see!" demanded Joyce, pushing her aside to peer at the photograph which showed a group of girls clad in breeches and woolly sweaters, with shawls

16

tied round them, and their hair, for the most part, tucked away in berets. They wore big, hob-nailed climbing-boots, and fingerless mittens, and looked very happy and jolly. Gillian pointed out the one whose face had taken her fancy—a slim, fair person, with a merry smile.

"I don't think she's so awfully pretty," said Joyce when she had considered it. "And I loathe the idea of those boots. They must make your feet look enormous!" And she glanced down at her own small feet in their pretty buckled slippers.

"They are very necessary in snowy weather, though, Miss Vanity," said their mother, running her fingers through the golden curls Joyce always wore floating loosely about her shoulders at home.

"I like this one of the library," said Gillian, turning it. "What piles of books!"

"The garden in summer looks ripping," commented Joyce. "Turn to that one again, Gill."

Gillian turned to the picture which showed a flower-garden with the girls sitting about in deck-chairs or on the grass, which the house itself showed in the background.

"Then you think you can be happy there?" asked their mother wistfully, when at length they put the pamphlet away.

"*Rather!*" said Joyce with conviction. "It looks a ripping place, and there are sure to be nice girls at a school like that. Won't it be funny, though, having lessons in French and German? I hope they'll make allowances for us at first. They ought to; they must know we can't be expected to know very much about it when we've never left England before."

"I wonder what their standard is like?" said Gillian thoughtfully.

"A pretty high one from all I can hear," said her mother. "One of the present Seniors hopes to enter the Sorbonne—the Paris University—in September, and that means that she must be very well advanced indeed. And they have sent girls to the universities here, so Lady

Talbot told me. I don't think you need trouble about their standard."

But Joyce's face had lengthened at this. "Oh, Mummy!"

"Well, my lazy baby, don't you like the prospect?" asked her mother, laughing. "Oh, of course you'll have to work! You can't go through life shirking trouble all your days."

"And there's one thing, Joyce," added Gillian. "You'll have regular hours there for prep and practice, and I believe you'll find it much easier to do your work that way than just messing about at home as you do."

"It's all very well for you," said Joyce petulantly. "You like work; I don't!—Mummy! Write and tell them I'm not to be pushed, won't you? I'm sure it would be bad for me."

Mrs. Linton shook her head. "They won't push you, Joyce. They are far too careful of the girls for that. But you'll have to do a certain amount of work, you know. Still, I don't think they'll ask too much of you."

"Well, won't you write to the High and say I must stop Latin and maths?" pleaded Joyce.

"Didn't you understand, dear? You aren't going back there again."

"Not going back? *Mummy!* How joyous!" And Joyce sprang up and began to dance about the room with delight.

"But, Mummy; what about our books?" asked Gillian, who was by no means so delighted at the prospect. She had always got on well with the mistresses, and she had one or two friends who lived outside the suburb, coming in to school every day. If she were not to go back, how could she say good-bye to them?

"Oh, yes; you may go for your books and to say good-bye to your friends," replied Mrs. Linton with a smile. "Joyce, stop dancing like that, you mad child. Aren't you sorry to leave your friends?"

Joyce subsided. "Oh, yes. But then I expect I'll make

18

others in this new school. When do we go to the Tyrol? And where is it?"

"*Joyce!* What shameful ignorance! It is the western part of Austria. Go and get your atlas and find it. As to when we go, it will be next week, I hope. And now, here comes Eva with supper.—Clear the table, Gill—and Joyce, go and brush your hair. It looks both wild and woolly after that war-dance of yours."

It was a bright day in the middle of December that they set off for Dover to make the first stage of their journey.

"You must take all the care of your mother that you can," said Dr. Talbot to Gillian, with whom he had a chat before they left. "Of course, Nurse will be there to see to most things; but you can do much."

Gillian turned wistful eyes of sapphire-blue on him. "She—she isn't—really bad?—is she?" she asked brokenly.

"I hope she will be better soon," he said evasively. "But remember; she is not to be worried. A great deal depends on that."

Gillian nodded. "I'll do everything I can. And so will Joyce, I'm sure," she added.

The doctor was not so sure. He had already sized up the younger girl, and it seemed to him that most of the burden must fall on this anxious-looking elder child. "Well, be careful," he said gruffly. "Remember that it will take time for her to get back her strength, and don't worry her by seeming impatient. *Your* cheerfulness will go a long way towards bringing her through."

After that he said good-bye, and left them in charge of the excellent nurse who would take them out to the Sonnalpe, see Mrs. Linton established at the Sanatorium, and then return. Nurse Richards had done this journey before, and she knew exactly what arrangements to make. They were to cross to Calais that day if it was smooth, and there spend the night, going on to Paris next morning.

19

From Paris, they would journey as far as Basle, where another break would be made for the sake of the invalid. The next stage would be at Innsbruck; and the final one to the Sonnalpe itself. Altogether they would be at least a week on the way, and the chances were that it would be more. Very much depended on how Mrs. Linton stood the travelling.

Joyce was the only really carefree member of the party. She knew that her mother was ill; but she had no idea how ill, for Mrs. Linton had begged that her youth might not be overshadowed by it. Gillian, accustomed to shielding her sister from everything, acquiesced at once, and so it was not till they had reached Paris, and Mrs. Linton was quietly resting in the pleasant room which had been taken for her at the Home established by an enterprising Scottish doctor for this very purpose, that the younger girl knew very much of what was happening. Then Nurse took matters into her own hands.

Joyce had been clamouring to go out and explore Paris, and Gillian, secretly terrified at the exhaustion she had seen in their mother's face, refused with decision.

"I think you're horrid!" cried Joyce. "It won't help Mummy a bit if we sit and mope and grizzle; and you might think of *me* a little!"

Gillian flushed up, but before she could reply, Nurse struck in firmly. "Look here, young woman, I think it's high time you knew just how things stand with you three."

"What do you mean?" demanded Joyce, half-alarmed, half-angry.

"Just this. Your mother is very ill—it's going to be a business to get her to the Sonnalpe, and your sister knows it. It's up to you to help in every way you can—and that won't be by whingeing and whining because you can't do everything as you like. You've got to keep bright and cheerful, and do all you can to cheer your mother up. And try to think a little more of other people, and less of yourself."

Joyce listened to her in stunned silence. She had really had no idea that her mother was so ill. Nurse had given her a shrewd blow from which she would not recover swiftly. Gillian, with the old instinct for protecting her sister, slipped an arm round her; but Joyce shook herself free.

"Is this true?" she demanded.

"Yes," said Nurse. "Now I must go to my patient. You two stay here quietly. Supper will be coming presently, and then you must go to bed."

She left the room, and when she had gone, Joyce flung round on her sister. "How long have you known all this?" she demanded imperiously.

"I've only *known* it for the last two or three days," said Gillian quietly. "I *guessed* it when I first heard we were to go to the Tyrol so that Mummy could have mountain air."

"And you never told *me*!"

"Mummy didn't want you to know till you had to."

Joyce stood still, her breath coming quickly. "Well, I think it's abominable of you to have kept such a thing secret from me," she said stormily. "I'm going to my bedroom—don't come with me; I want to be alone! Anyhow, I don't want anyone with me who could behave like such a beast as you!"

She turned and fled from the room, banging the door behind her, and Gillian was left gasping at her sister's fury. Up the stairs rushed the frightened child, and into the bedroom she was to share with her sister. Mercifully, it was on the floor below their mother's and nowhere near her. Nor was there anyone else within hearing—which was as well, for once she had gained it, Joyce slammed the door, flung herself on the bed, and cried passionately and noisily. She loved her mother as dearly as she could love anyone but herself, and Nurse's blunt statements had terrified her. Besides, there was a good deal of wounded vanity in her crying, for Nurse had not troubled to hide the contempt she felt.

21

It was a good thing, as it turned out, that Nurse had spoken, for her patient was not fit to go on next day, and as the weather was bad, the two girls had to amuse themselves as best they could for the next two days. But at length there came a sunshiny morning when Mrs. Linton was laid in an ambulance, and taken to the Gare de l'Est, where she was put into a compartment specially reserved for her, and they went on to Basle. But there again they had to make a break, and it was very slow work. Finally, when they arrived at the little station of Wiesing, they had been more than a fortnight on the way. Christmas had come and gone, and the new year had arrived.

Two attendants from the Sanatorium were in waiting at Wiesing, and they swiftly wrapped up the half-fainting patient, and carried her out to the motor ambulance which was waiting outside in the falling twilight of the winter afternoon. Nurse followed them, bidding Gillian and Joyce stay where they were till someone came for them. A third man went off to see about the luggage, and the two girls huddled together on the lamplit platform, cold, hungry, and miserable, and very lonely and desolate. However, just as Gillian was summoning up the little German she knew to speak to the luggage attendant, things changed. There came the sound of light, swift steps, and a tall, very dark girl, with thick black hair cut in a "page's" bob under her fur cap, and soft black eyes set in a pointed face, came whirling up to them with outstretched hands.

"You poor lambs!" she said. "I'm sorry we left you so long, but your mother had to come first, of course. Now which is Gillian and which is Joyce? I'm Jo Bettany, by the way, head-girl of the Chalet School. My sister married Dr. Russell who is head of the Sonnalpe, and Dr. Maynard and I came down to welcome you to Tyrol and take you up there. You're coming to us at 'Die Rosen'— my sister's home—till term begins, you know. Has Louis got all your luggage? Then come along, and we'll soon have you at home now. You must be sick of travelling."

She slipped a hand through an arm of each girl, and

chatting and laughing, drew them out of the station to a car which was driven by a big young man with a fair, clear-cut face under his ear-flapped fur cap. This was Dr. Maynard, who gave them a cheery greeting, and helped Jo to tuck them in. Then he set off at once through the lighted streets of the little town to the foot of the broad carriage-road, where, far away in the distance, they could see the tail-lights of the ambulance twinkling.

"We go up here," said Jo, turning to the pair. "This leads up to the Sonnalpe, though it's at the far end. The village is right round the shoulder of the mountain, as you'll find when we get there."

"Where are they taking Mummy?" asked Gillian, finding her voice at last. "We must go where she is, of course."

Jo looked at her with eyes grown very soft and tender. "You can't go yet, at any rate," she said. "They're taking her to the San. You must come with us to 'Die Rosen.' But you needn't be afraid. As soon as ever we get there, my sister will ring up the San and find out how your mother is, and you shall see her as soon as possible."

Gillian nodded. Then she lay back under the great fur-lined rug that had been tucked round them. She could feel tired Joyce nodding against her; but she herself was very far from sleep. She had too much to think about.

CHAPTER III

AT THE SONNALPE

IT was a slow journey up the broad driving-road. Snow lay thickly everywhere, and even the chains on the wheels would have been little safeguard against fast or careless driving. Luckily Dr. Maynard was accustomed to the work, and by degrees they mounted to the top, always with the lights of the ambulance before them, and then Gillian felt that they were running along an even path.

"This is the Sonnalpe itself," said Joey. "I do hope you're quite warm and comfortable? Dr. Jack daren't go quickly, you see—not in this weather, anyhow. You've been a long time on the way, haven't you? We all thought you'd have been here much sooner."

Gillian roused herself with an effort. "Mummy was too poorly for us to come quicker."

"That's a pity," said Joey quietly. "Still, she's here now, and that's the main thing. You know, don't you, that her doctor wrote to my brother-in-law about her?"

"No; I'd no idea. Oh, do you know what he said?" Gillian turned with some eagerness at this, though hitherto her remarks had been mechanical.

Jo shook her head. "What do you take Jem for? Doctors aren't in the habit of confiding to even their nearest and dearest, my child. I do know she's very ill, of course. And my sister says that your doctor's wife who wrote to her about you two said that this was her best chance. She'll get the very newest treatment up here, you know. You mustn't mind if they don't let you see her to-night. She'll be pretty well done with the journey, and they're safe to want her to rest. You see, before they can begin any treatment they'll have to build up her strength.

24

I know! My little adopted sister, the Robin, is fearfully frail, and I know all the fussations we have over her."

Gillian nodded. Then, as she saw that they were approaching houses, she leaned forward to look out of the window.

"Yes; this is the village," said Joey. She pointed out of the window at her side. "There's the San—that huge building looming up over there. You can see by the lights that the ambulance is turning in. We shall go on though, to my sister's house."

Gillian suddenly remembered her manners. "It's ripping of Mrs. Russell to take us in like this," she said. "I never expected it, you know. Quite thought we'd have to camp out in some hotel or other."

"Oh, Madge wouldn't let people like you go to the hotel if it could be helped," said Jo cheerfully. "And even if we hadn't been able to take you, there are the Mensches and the Di Bersettis. Both Frau Mensch and Signora di Bersetti are old girls of the Chalet School, and it isn't likely they'd let new Chalet girls go to the 'Goldener Apfel' unless we'd mumps or measles or something like that."

At this point, they turned in at a wide gateway, and the car went slowly up the pathway which was bordered on either hand by bushes laden with snow. From the windows lights fell athwart the white garden in a welcoming golden glow, and as Dr. Maynard sounded his horn, the big front door was flung wide open, and more lights streamed out to greet them. A slender figure appeared at the doorway, and a hand was waved from beneath the great shawl that wrapped the figure from throat to knee.

"My sister!" said Jo, wrenching at the handle of the car-door. "Come along; we're here at last. Oh, is Joyce asleep?"

But Joyce had roused up with the stopping of the car, and was lifting her head with an air of bewilderment.

"We're here, Joyce," said Gillian, shaking her gently. "Get out, dear."

25

Joyce stumbled out, blinking and yawning, and still too drowsy to assert herself. Joey seized her hand. and pulled her up the long, shallow steps to the door. "Here they are!" she cried. "This is Joyce; and that's Gillian coming behind!"

Warm hands were stretched to grasp theirs, and they were drawn into the well-lighted hall, which was summer-warm and sweet with the perfume of hothouse flowers. A sweet voice said, "At last! You poor children! You must be worn-out, and half-starved! Come along and take off your things, and get thawed out."

They were taken to a little cloakroom where Joey gave them pegs, helped them to get rid of their wraps, and discarded her own. They had slippers in their little hand-case, and there was plenty of hot water, so they were able to freshen themselves considerably. Then she led them across the hall and into a wide, lofty room, where a great porcelain stove filled up one corner, and sent a rosy glow half-way across the floor; stands filled with flowering plants stood beside the walls, and bookcases, crammed with books, ran down one side. The electric lights were shaded with orange shades, and, best of all to the two tired travellers, a table arranged for a meal stood near the stove. Behind the table was a couch, on which sprawled a slight girl in the early twenties, while an invalid-chair holding a fair girl of about Gillian's age, and a little stool on which sat a child of ten or eleven were set near the armchair occupied by Mrs. Russell.

The grown-up girl got up as they came in, and came to greet them. "Welcome to 'Die Rosen,'" she said with a smile. "I'm Grizel Cochrane—an old girl of the Chalet School, and now music mistress at the Annexe up here. This is Stacie Benson, one of our girls, who is recovering from an accident. And here is our Robin." And she stretched out a slim, long-fingered hand to ruffle the black curls that clustered all over the Robin's small head.

"This is Joyce," said Gillian, guessing that Joyce was, for once in her life, shy, "and I'm Gillian."

"Come and sit down," said Mrs. Russell, who had risen with Grizel and the Robin. "Robinette, run and ask Rosa to bring in Kaffee, mein Blümchen. Gillian and Joyce must be half-starved by this time."

The little girl slipped out of the room, and the two strangers sat down, Joyce still very quiet, and Gillian beginning to realise how tired she was.

"Did you come along all right, Jo—" asked Grizel Cochrane, feeling that it would be kindest to leave them to recover themselves a little.

Jo nodded. "Very slow, of course. Couldn't be anything else with such snow and frost.—By the way, Madge, Jack's gone back to the San. He asked me to tell you. Are the babies all in bed?"

"All in bed and asleep," replied her sister with a smile. "Robin must go very soon; it must be nearly nineteen now. I wish that clock hadn't begun to gain like this. It's most awkward with my watch out of action as well."

"Ah, you want Evvy and Co. to put that clock right," said Jo, with a wicked grin at Stacie. "They'd soon have her going!"

"Thanks! I'd rather be excused," retorted Mrs. Russell decidedly. "Ah, here comes Rosa! Now you two shall have something to keep you going till Abendessen, which won't occur for an hour and a half."

Rosa, a dumpy, flaxen-haired Tyrolean, with broad, beaming face, came in, bearing the prettily arranged tray with its milky coffee and a basket full of twists of fancy-bread. A mug of rich milk was there also, for the Robin whose supper time this was. They all gathered round the table, for Jo announced herself as famished, and the others were not averse to an extra cup of coffee. Perhaps Gillian was the only one to be lacking in enthusiasm. She was too anxious for news of her mother to relish even the dainty meal spread for them. However, Joey, after exchanging a glance with her sister, murmured, "Excuse me, please," and vanished. She returned a few minutes later, beaming.

"Well?" asked her sister. "What news, Jo?"

27

"Quite good," said Jo. She turned to Gillian and Joyce. "I've just rung up the San. The news is that your mother has been got comfortably to bed. She's had some soup, and now she is settling off to sleep quite nicely. They say she is quite happy about you, and seems inclined to settle in an once, which is just what they want, of course."

"Who spoke?" asked Stacie.

"Gottfried did. Jem is still with Mrs. Linton, and won't leave her till she is asleep. But Gottfried had just left her, so he knew the latest, of course. You'll feel quite happy about her now, won't you?" And she turned to Gillian again, who was biting her lips to keep back the sobs that were rising in her throat.

Joyce, however, was still rather vague about her mother's illness, so was less affected. "That's ripping news!" she said. "I say, ta awfully for asking!"

The elders exchanged glances at this flow of slang, but they could scarcely pull her up for it at once.

"Besides," said Jo when the younger girls had all gone to bed and they were alone, "it isn't term-time yet."

"All the same, she must learn to speak purer English than that," said Mrs. Russell. "I don't want the Robin to pick up such expressions, you know."

However, at the time, nothing was said, and Joyce was complacently ignorant of the sin she had committed. She began to forget her shyness, and turned to Stacie as being the most interesting person there, because the nearest to her own age. "I say, what sort of an accident did you have?" she asked. "Won't you ever be able to walk again?"

"Of course she will!" said Joey sharply. "It was a sprained muscle in her back, and we've had such hot weather that it's made her recovery slow. But she's going ahead like a steam-engine now."

Joyce glanced at her curiously. She was quite devoid of either tact or intuition, but she could see that what she had just said had upset Jo, so she dropped the subject and leaned back in her chair with a little air of languor.

28

"I think the heat in here is making me sleepy. I can scarcely keep my eyes open."

"Perhaps you would like to go to bed when the Robin goes?" suggested Mrs. Russell kindly. "We can send in your Abendessen on a tray, you know."

"Oh, Joyce isn't as tired as all that," said Gillian hastily, turning red as she spoke. How *awful* Joyce was! As if they could start giving trouble that way in a strange house!

And Joyce herself was by no means pleased with the idea. She wanted to see Dr. Russell, and she was not minded to let Gillian have a better chance of making friends than herself. "Oh, I'm not so tired really," she said. "It's only the warmth after coming in from the cold."

"Just as you like, dear," said Madge Russell.

"Oh, I can sit up quite easily. Gill was right about that," said Joyce graciously.

"Gill—is that how you abbreviate your name?" asked Mrs. Russell. "It's a very pretty one, and quite uncommon, Gillian, dear."

"Mummy read it in a book," Joyce informed the company. "She was so thrilled with it, that when Gill landed along a bit later, she shoved it on to her. Of course, *I* am christened after her. Daddy insisted on it."

"Yes; it's a pretty name, too. But I should think you'll get a dozen Joyces to one Gillian," said Jo bluntly.

Then the Robin created a diversion by jumping up and announcing that she must say good-night. She was hugged and kissed all round, Mrs. Russell promising to come up presently to hear her prayers and tuck her in. Then she came across to the Lintons, her face lifted for the kiss she confidently expected from them. Gillian gave it at once. Joyce, after a wide-eyed stare, tossed her a careless nod, and said, "Oh, night-night, kid!"

The Robin trotted away serenely; but Joyce had scored herself a black mark from Joey Bettany. The Robin was everybody's pet, and only her remarkably sweet nature could have saved her from being spoilt. In the short eleven years of her life she had met with nothing but petting and love. and Jo was inclined to take it as a personal insult if anyone showed any sign of giving the child anything else. But Miss Joyce was a spoilt baby herself, and she resented the adoration that was obviously showered on the younger child.

After all, the Lintons were fated not to meet Dr. Russell that night, for he rang up shortly before Abendessen to say that he would not be home till much later. Mrs. Russell said nothing much to the girls. She was too much occupied in hoping that it was not Mrs. Linton's condition which kept him at the Sanatorium. After the meal was over, Stacie and Joyce went off to bed, and Gillian, who owned to feeling very sleepy, followed not long after. Then Jo Bettany pulled up a little stool beside her sister's chair, while Grizel Cochrane departed to her own room to write letters, for the postman would be up in the morning on his bi-weekly visit to collect all mail.

Madge Russell, coming back from a visit to her young guests to see that they had all they required, and having had a peep in at the night-nursery where her twin nephew and niece were sound asleep at one side of the room, while her own small son was curled up in his cot at the other, found her young sister in sole possession of the salon and awaiting her return eagerly.

"Come along and pow-wow!" she said as the mistress of the house entered.

"Very well. But just remember, Jo that it's far too early to judge yet," said Mrs. Russell, as she sat down and took up her sewing.

"I know. But still, they've given themselves away quite a good deal, *I* think," said Jo with an omniscient wag of her black head. "What do *you* think of them, Madge?"

"I like Gillian," said Madge decidedly. "She has any amount of character in her. Poor child! She's obviously very anxious and distressed about her mother! We must try to keep her from thinking about it if we can."

30

"That won't be very easy," said Jo with a frown. "She's rather the kind that worries things to shreds, I should think. Isn't she pretty, with her black hair and blue eyes, and that rose-leafy kind of skin? Just like the Irish heroines in books!"

"Very pretty. Of course, Joyce is the family beauty, though."

"Yes; what price that Joyce-child?"

"She's only a baby, really. And she certainly is exceedingly pretty, Jo."

"*And* knows it! I should say myself that she's chock-full of conceit!" said Jo uncharitably.

"I expect they have spoilt her at home," said Madge. "And she has rather charming manners, too."

"Can't say I saw much of them myself. I thought she was a loathsome little wretch."

"Jo, you simply must get over this silly dislike of everyone who doesn't instantly fall down before the Robin," said Madge severely.

"Oh, it wasn't only that. Didn't you notice what she said to Stacie? Poor old Stacie doesn't want things rubbed in any more than has happened already—and certainly not by a conceited little ape of fourteen!"

"That was mere thoughtlessness," said Madge. "And you must remember, Jo, that we are accustomed to all this sort of thing. I imagine that Joyce Linton has been sheltered from all the unpleasant side of life in every possible way."

"She made Gillian jolly uncomfortable by saying she was tired like that," remarked Jo.

"I know. But there, again, it was only thoughtlessness. In any case, Jo, do give the child a fair chance. If you had been travelling for days on end, I doubt if you would have shown up much better than Joyce. Give her two or three days with us after she's rested and refreshed, and just see if she isn't as nice as most girls are."

Jo subsided with a grunt, but she was by no means satisfied. However, as her sister presently suggested that it was high time she went to bed, the conversation ended for the time being, and was not resumed for a considerable period; and then a good many things had happened.

CHAPTER IV

THE CHALET SCHOOL REOPENS

"Joey—Joey! Mademoiselle wants you at once!"

Joey Bettany stopped half-way up the stairs, and turned round to look at the messenger, a slim, curly-headed girl of fifteen. "Where is she, Evvy?"

"In the study. Guess you're coming over a bit thick, aren't you?" retorted Evvy, with a faint accent that proclaimed her American.

Jo marched down the stairs again. "Don't be rude, my child, even if this *is* only first day. Any idea what she wants?"

"None at all. Guess you'll find out when you get there."

Jo heaved a sigh and went slowly along the passage and tapped at a door near the front-door. A pleasant voice said, "Entrez!" and she went in to curtsey to Mademoiselle Lepâttre, the acting Head of the school, and Mrs. Russell's co-partner.

"Evadne says you wish to speak to me, Mademoiselle," said the head-girl as she closed the door behind her.

Mademoiselle looked up from the big plan on her desk. There was a slight frown on her plain, though pleasant face, and Jo promptly began to ransack her memory for any escapade of hers that might have brought it there. She could think of nothing, and Mademoiselle began to explain next moment.

"Pray sit down, Joey. I wish to discuss something with you."

Jo sat down, and composed her features into something resembling the dignity incumbent on a head-girl who is discussing matters with the head-mistress. "Yes, Mademoiselle?" she said, using the French Mademoiselle had been speaking.

"It is about those two new girls, Gillian and Joyce Linton," said Mademoiselle. "Have you been told that the ceiling of the Carnation dormitory has fallen down?"

Jo went scarlet, especially as the mistress went on, "I cannot think why this should have happened; but it has rendered the room useless for the present. Fortunately, as we have rearranged matters at Le Petit Chalet, we can do without it just now. I had intended placing Gillian and Joyce in it with Cornelia Flower as head. Cornelia, I am sending upstairs to the Violet dormitory, but I am not very sure what to do with the new girls."

Jo was too well trained to make any comments, but she felt rather bewildered at all this. What on earth had *she* to do with dormitory arrangements? These were the concern of Mademoiselle and Matron.

"You see," went on the Head, "there is another bed in the Violet dormitory, and also one in the Amber. What I cannot decide is whether to place Greta Macdonald in the Amber, and so leave Joyce and Gillian together in the Violet; or whether to separate them. We know why they are here, of course; and we know how very serious matters are likely to be for them. And you, Joey, know the two girls, whereas I have only met them now. Therefore I wish you to say which you think would be kinder—to let them be together, or to separate them."

"I see." Joey frowned horribly over the problem. She knew which she would have preferred. The week spent in the company of the Lintons had confirmed her in her opinion of both of them. She liked Gillian, and thought Joyce detestably conceited and selfish, even though she owned that the child had some reason for her conceit. It must be confessed that, with the sole exceptions of the beloved little Robin, her own great friend Marie von Eschenau, and Marie's sister, now Wanda von Gluck, she had never seen a prettier girl. Joyce's perfect little face

34

with its aureole of golden curls and big, azure-blue eyes, would have rejoiced the heart of any artist. But Joey didn't like her any the better for it.

"I'd separate them, I think, Mademoiselle," she said at length. "Joyce will be better with girls of her own age. And if Gillian is away from her, then the change may help her not to brood over things."

Mademoiselle nodded. "You consider, then, that Joyce will not fret if she is parted from her elder sister?"

"No; I don't think so," said Jo, repressing the first emphatic disclaimer which had sprung to her lips.

"Very well. I will put Joyce with Cornelia and Greta and Violet; and Gillian shall go to the Amber dormitory with Cyrilla Maurús, Elsie Carr, and Amalie Hamel. It is strange," she went on meditatively. "I cannot account for that ceiling falling like this."

If she had not been entering the names on the dormitories chart, she would have seen that once more Joey was scarlet. *She* could guess, all too accurately, at the cause for the collapse of that ceiling. On the last night of the previous term, when all rules were in abeyance, she had been moved to organise a circus among the Seniors; and the resultant bumps and bangs as they turned somersaults or tried to walk on their hands were quite sufficient to have brought down any ceiling. Luckily for her, Mademoiselle took no notice of her for a moment, and by the time the lady looked up, she was normal hue again.

"That will be all, then, Joey. But pray bid all in the Green dormitory to tread lightly. We do not desire any accidents."

Joey got up at this dismissal. "Yes, Mademoiselle," she said dutifully. She went to the door, opened it, and before departing, turned to make her curtsey again. Then she backed out, and nearly fell over Joyce Linton, who had been watching her, open-mouthed.

"D'you mean to say we've got to bob like that?" demanded the younger girl when both had recovered their balance again.

35

"Certainly," said Jo, suddenly becoming the complete head-girl.

"Holy smoke!" ejaculated Joyce somewhat vulgarly.

Joey was down on her like a flash. "Look here, Joyce, I don't want to begin to find fault with you already, but slang of that kind isn't allowed here. If you think it over, you'll see why. We have a good many girls who aren't English, and their people won't thank us if they go home using slang—and vulgar slang at that!—and then say they learnt it here. If you use it, you'll soon find yourself minus your pocket-money. This is first day, when rules are relaxed a little, and I'm telling you now so that you'll have due warning."

She moved away, and Joyce stared for a moment before she suddenly ran after her. "I say! Just a sec! You surely don't mean all that rigmarole you got off your chest just now?"

"Every word of it," said Jo solemnly. "You'll get fined for every forbidden word you use."

"Help!" Joyce's jaw dropped. "At that rate, it strikes me I'd better come over dumb for the rest of the term!"

Jo laughed. "Oh, it won't be as bad as all that. You'll remember when you've been penniless a week or two."

"But they don't cabbage all your cash for just an odd word or two?" persisted Joyce, still incredulous.

"Depends on the words. If it's what the authorities call slang, then yes, they will. A groschen for every word; and out of two schillings, that soon leaves you minus any money."

"How simply ghastly!"

Jo nodded to her, and then went off to her own quarters, while Joyce, after thinking it over, went her way to the big common-room where several of the Middles were congregated, and sought out a certain bright-haired American, Cornelia Flower by name, to find out from her if such things could really be.

"Guess that's right, all right," said Cornelia when she

36

had heard what the new girl had to say. "*I* ought to know!"

"You certainly ought, Corney!" laughed a pretty, dark-haired girl of fifteen. "You and Evvy have contributed a fair amount to the fines-box in your time."

"But how putrid!" said Joyce. "What awful rot!"

Cornelia proceeded to jump on her—heavily, too. "It isn't rot! It's only common-sense."

"Hullo! Is Saul also among the prophets?" demanded the dark girl teasingly. "Imagine such sentiments from you of all people!"

Cornelia blushed. "Oh, I know I've been awful," she confessed. "All the same it isn't rot, and we don't want any new girls coming here saying so."

"Oh, sorry!" said Joyce after a long, cool stare. "I can see I shall have to be dumb, that's all."

"Oh, you'll soon remember," they chorused.

Joyce said no more, and presently they left her while they went to greet a fresh batch of arrivals. She didn't like this, for at the High School she had always been surrounded by a mob of adoring followers. What was more, so far no one had shown any signs of wanting to follow her. She didn't like it at all. She didn't like these girls who were so friendly together, and who treated her with courtesy, it is true, but in such a way that she felt herself something of an outsider. As for Jo Bettany, she felt that she positively detested *her*. Jo was not a great deal more tactful than Joyce herself, and she had not troubled to hide the fact that she didn't think much of the younger Linton.

At this moment, Gillian came into the room together with a sturdily-built girl of her own age, whose long brown hair hung in two thick pigtails on either shoulder. Joyce wondered who she was, and felt half-envious of her sister, who was laughing and chatting with this stranger. The Middles to whom she had been speaking about the slang fines now returned, chased from the corridors by Matron, who had no desire to start the term with a batch of bad colds, and joined the pair. Joyce heard her sister's companion addressed as "Lonny," and wondered idly what it stood for. Then there was a little stir, and a breaking-up of the groups as some newcomers came in. Gillian looked round, saw her sister by herself, and came over to speak to her.

"Here you are," she said. "I wondered where you were. Isn't this a top-hole place?"

"You haven't to use words like that," Joyce informed her.

"Words like what?"

"Oh, top-hole, and so on. They fine you if you do. Jo Bettany has just been telling me, and so have those girls!" And she indicated a noisy group over by the stove.

"Oh, my goodness!" Gillian was almost as taken aback as her sister.

"Yes; isn't it the pink limit? I'll have to be dumb if I want to have any cash, for I certainly can't remember things like that."

"It will be frightfully difficult." Gillian looked worried. "I remember I tried to give it up for Lent one year, and it was simply awful."

"So you did!" Joyce began to laugh. "I don't see that it did much to improve you, old peach."

"Well, I suppose I must just have another shot. There's one thing, I don't believe it'll be quite so difficult here."

"How d'you make that out?"

"Well, no one else seems to use much. At the High, everyone did, and that was partly why it was so difficult."

"Don't you believe it! I think this looks like being a horrid school. At least they didn't expect you to talk like a prim Victorian ass at the High, and jump on you if you didn't."

"No; they didn't. But Mummy didn't like it much," said Gillian thoughtfully. "I remember she absolutely forbade us to say, 'Oh, yeh!' and 'Sez you!'"

"Well, I'm beginning to wish we'd gone to a boarding-

38

school in England. Then we wouldn't have been bothered this way."

"But we'd have been so far from Mummy," said Gillian.

"Mummy's all right. She'll soon be fit now. Look how blossoming she was when we went to say good-bye! I think there's been an awful fuss made for very little!"

Gillian turned a look of bitter reproach on her sister. "Joyce! How can you be so heartless? Mummy's jolly ill, let me tell you—heaps iller than she's even let us know. I think you're a regular little pig to talk of her like that!"

"Oh, don't try and come the good elder sister over me!" snapped Joyce. "If you're going to preach, I'm off!" And she turned and ran off, leaving Gillian staring after her.

It was at this point that she noticed a very tall, fair girl who had just come into the room as Joyce left it. She was greeted courteously but briefly, and there were none of the welcoming shouts that had greeted so many of the others. She held herself stiffly erect, and even when the ringing of a bell brought in maids in their pretty national costume, bearing great urns of milky coffee and baskets filled with bread-twists and cakes, most of the girls made for the basket-chairs, pulled into little groups about the room, without troubling about her particularly. Nor did she pay them much attention. She sat down near a group among which Gillian recognised the girl who had taken charge of her when they reached the school and who had been introduced as, "This is Lonny—I mean Ilonka Barkocz. She will look after you for the present."

Feeling very new, Gillian stood by shyly till Ilonka suddenly looked up and saw her standing by the window. She jumped up at once and came to her. "I did not know you were alone," she said in the careful English which bespoke her continental origin. "I thought you were with your sister."

"Joyce left me very soon," said Gillian shyly.

"Ah, I expect she has made friends of her own age,"

39

said Ilonka. "Will you come and sit with us, while we have Kaffee und Kuchen?"

Gillian had already learned that this was the synonym for the meal which, in this land, took the place of afternoon tea. She warmed to Ilonka's friendliness, and accompanied her to the group, where she was introduced all round.

"Girls, I bring you a new friend. This is Gillian Linton who will be with us in the Fifth, Joey says.—Gillian, these are some of the girls in our form."

"Glad you've come, Gillian," said a girl of Gillian's own age, with a bright, interesting face which told of great force of character. "I'm Margia Stevens; Lonny you know —this is Elsie Carr."

"In your form too," laughed the pretty dark girl who had been with Cornelia before. "Hope you aren't *too* brilliant at work, Gillian—especially science.—This on my left hand is Evadne Lannis—known to the police as 'Evvy.' *She* is really good, now!—treats us to explosions and fireworks and things of that kind!"

A chuckle went round the group, and Evadne flushed to the roots of her fair curls. "Don't be such a mean, Elsie Carr!" she cried. "I'd just despise to be all that catty!"

Elsie laughed. "Then you shouldn't get up sensations, my child! But I'm introducing Gillian. Let me finish.— This is Cyrilla Maurús, Gillian, who is Hungarian like Lonny.—And these are Giovanna Donati and Hilda Bhaer. —and this Thekla von Stift," and she indicated the tall fair girl with a wave of her hand. "Now sit down, and Cyrilla and I will go and scrounge coffee for four.—Two of you folk come and help. Here come the prees."

Gillian looked towards the door, and saw nine girls headed by Jo Bettany, coming into the room. She liked the looks of them at once. Jo she knew already and was beginning to admire with all her heart. The little dark girl with the black hair (which was obviously a "bob" growing long) had already been introduced to her as Simone Lecoutier. She had no idea who the others were, but she

40

decided that they compared very favourably with the prefects at the High School. Then Elsie came back with a cup of coffee for her, and Giovanna offered her a bread-twist, and they all sat laughing and chatting, even Thekla joining in now and then when they addressed her. In the opposite corner Gillian could see Joyce with one or two girls of her own age, and felt happy about her again. After all, Joyce was a dreadful baby for fourteen, and she would soon shake down. So the elder girl thought in the intervals of listening to the school gossip and answering such questions as they addressed to her.

After Kaffee und Kuchen the girls hurried to clear the room and set the chairs in straight rows, for they always had Assembly there on the first night of term, when Mademoiselle came in to bid them formal welcome and to tell them any news. A good many were called off by Matron to unpack; but the Lintons and Jo had been among the earliest comers, and had finished long ago. So they were called to help Joey and her three friends, Simone Lecoutier, Marie von Eschenau, and Frieda Mensch, to make the room ready.

"For goodness' sake see that the lines are straight!" said Jo as she tore off in answer to a summons from Margia Stevens.—"All right! I'm coming!"

"Do you think you shall like the school?" asked Simone Lecoutier of Gillian as they worked.

"I expect so," said Gillian cautiously.

Frieda Mensch smiled at her. "Oh, you will like it," she said in the soft, pretty voice Gillian had already noticed and admired in her. "Everyone does."

"Not Thekla," said Marie von Eschenau gloomily. "She has come back almost as bad as when she first came."

Gillian looked curiously at Marie, whose loveliness seemed to her to exceed even Joyce's. "Thekla is that tall girl who sat near us at tea-time—I mean Kaffee—isn't she?" she asked.

"Yes; she is my cousin," Marie informed her, still gloomily.

"Don't you like her?" asked Joyce inquisitively, as her work brought her up to them in time to hear Marie's remark.

"She is not like the rest of us," said Marie shortly. "Bring some more chairs, please."

It was quite plain that she was going to say no more, and Joyce shrugged her shoulders and went to do as she was told. But her curiosity was aroused, and when Thekla had finished unpacking and returned to the room, she looked at her consideringly. She was rather impressed by the elder girl's supercilious airs, for Joyce was empty-headed enough, and Thekla's evident feeling of superiority made her think that here was someone who would be worth knowing. She looked at her again, and then turned to watch Marie as she set chairs for the Staff. Joyce had been the prettiest girl in her old school, and had thoroughly enjoyed queening it. She was by no means delighted to find on her arrival at this school that there was a girl who could certainly rival her in appearance. That it should be one older than herself made it no better. Joyce had had experience of the way in which younger girls run after older ones, and she was not content to be second.

Meanwhile, Marie, with no idea of the feeling she was arousing in the new girl's heart, finished her work, and then advised Joyce and Gillian to go and wash their hands. She showed them where to go, and vanished upstairs to rearrange her own flowing golden curls, which she wore tied back with a broad brown ribbon, the school colour. Jo was in the dormitory when she entered, finishing off odds and ends.

"All ready?" asked the head-girl.

"Quite," said Marie. "But I must brush my hair, Joey. The bell will go soon."

It went two minutes later, and the girls streamed into the common-room from all quarters of the house. From Le Petit Chalet came the Juniors, escorted by their own mistresses, and the prefects hastened down from the prefects' room where they had been discussing various

42

things. Cornelia Flower showed Joyce where to sit, and Cyrilla Maurús took Gillian under her wing. They were the only new girls this term, and the rest knew their places. Then the low-voiced chatter which had been going on was hushed as the door at the top of the room opened, and Mademoiselle came in, followed by the Staff.

She promised them only a short speech that evening. First, she bade them welcome, and reminded them that this was the term when they held their annual bazaar in aid of the free beds in the great Sanatorium at the Sonnalpe.

"We want to make our bazaar larger than ever this term," she said, "so I trust that all will work with a will. You will have your usual activities this term—Guides, Hobbies Club, and Pets. We hope that you will be able to arrange an entertainment to take place when we have our bazaar; and here and now the Staff invite you all to an evening's pleasure on an early Saturday in February.

"And now I wish to speak of something different. As some of you may remember, it was decided that we should add a Domestic Economy department to the school this term. That has been made possible through the generosity of Dr. Russell and our dear Madame. Two of the big sheds at the back of this house have been turned into kitchen and laundry, and there we hope that you will learn the secrets of la cuisine, and will, if you should go into camp as Guides this summer, be able to launder your garments yourselves with great success. Many other things will be taught there besides; for while we wish you to become cultured women, we also desire that you shall be home-makers. So the Seniors and the Middles will take it in turns to spend a day each week in the kitchens, and there learn all that our new mistress, Frau Mieders, can teach you of these matters. At present we shall not begin until Monday, when the Sixth Form will go to Frau Mieders. The Upper Fifth will go on Tuesday, and the Lower Fifth on Wednesday. On Thursday, the Fourth Form will take their turn, and the Third will go on Friday.

I hope you will all work well, and Miss Wilson tells me that she expects as many of you as possible to qualify for Cook's and Laundress' badges this term." Here she cast a laughing glance across at the tall, pleasant-faced mistress who sat at one end of the little dais.

Miss Wilson rose to the occasion. "It's high time you all had those badges, girls," she said. "I know we have a few; but I want to see every Guide with them."

"And finally," went on Mademoiselle, when Miss Wilson had sat down, "I wish to speak of Half-term. Those who wish to go home will do so, of course, and for the rest, we will provide as well as we can. But there will be no special occasion this term. Now that is all." She turned to Matron. "Matron, have all finished unpacking?"

"Not all, Mademoiselle," replied Matron.

"Then you will require those who have not, I know. They may go with you at once.—The rest may dance until the bell rings for Abendessen, which will be at twenty o'clock to-night. After that we will have Prayers, and then bed, for you must all be fatigued with your travelling. Thank you, mes enfants."

They stood while she and the Staff went out; and then Matron carried off her victims, and the rest took partners and began to dance the swift Viennese waltz to the accompaniment played by Anne Seymour, a pretty English girl of seventeen.

Gillian enjoyed it thoroughly, but she was glad when bedtime came for all that. She felt as if she had lived through so much since the morning. As for Joyce, she was inclined to rebel at the early bed, for at home Mrs. Linton had given way on that point, so that often it was ten and later before the girls went off. However, there was no appealing against it here, so she departed with her head full of schemes for making herself queen among her contemporaries, at least as much as ever she had been at the High School.

CHAPTER V

AN EARLY REBELLION

THE two Lintons settled down fairly quickly at the Chalet School. Gillian, placed in the Upper Fifth, soon made friends with the leaders of it. She was a keen worker, ready for most things, and, without having the personal charm which helped Joyce to queen it over most people, was very attractive. Joyce, on the other hand, was not having too easy a time. She made friends, for many of the girls fell under the thrall of her beauty and pretty manners. But the people she would have liked to acknowledge her were all too busy with their own concerns and too close friends already to welcome a new girl into their innermost circle. Such girls as Evadne Lannis and Cornelia Flower, for instance, took very little notice of her, and these two were decidedly leaders among their own set. She had to be content with the homage of lesser people such as Hilda Bhaer, Klara Melnarti, Kitty Burnett, Greta Macdonald, and Dorothy Brantham.

"Those Middles are starting a second party," said Anne Seymour to the rest of the Sixth, one snowy day at the end of January.

"If it's anything that will help to squash the activities of Evvy and Co, good luck to it! That's all I've got to say," yawned Jo Bettany as she opened her French grammar. "I never got a stroke of work done last night at prep. Really, considering that they are Fifth Form now, you'd think they'd try to develop a little sense. But that seems to be beyond them."

"What happened, my Jo?" asked Simone Lecoutier.

Jo groaned. "What *didn't* happen, you mean! To begin with, none of them had their geometry books. When I asked why, they blandly informed me that Charlie had them."

"But why?" asked Frieda Mensch, opening her eyes widely.

"I've no idea, and I didn't try to find out—Carla von Flügen, I believe you know something about it."

The Sixth with one accord turned to Carla von Flügen, who had been smiling in a way that certainly justified Jo's exclamation. "Naturally they would not explain," she said. "Charlie found them lying about ages after they should have been taken to Miss Leslie, and she confiscated them, and told Miss Leslie why."

"Well!" ejaculated Jo.

"I believe they got into terrible trouble about it with Miss Leslie," went on Carla, "for she was enraged about it."

"So well she might be! I only wonder Charlie let them have them."

"But that was not all, my Jo," insisted Simone, who had been watching her idol closely. "What else did they do?"

"Oh, go away and let me get some work done!" groaned Jo.

"Oh, nonsense!" laughed Anne. "It's a dull day, and, as head-girl, it's your duty to entertain us. Besides, this is free time."

"Precious lot of free time I get when you folk are about," grumbled Jo, giving up her attempts at work with a bang as she closed her book.

"Well, tell us what the Middles did," pleaded Sophie Hamel, a big Tyrolean, whose father was proprietor of a large drapery shop in Innsbruck.

Jo began to grin. "Oh, they began with the usual things —noughts-and-crosses; tilting their chairs; squeaking their pens. You know what they are like when they are bored."

"It is the not going out," said Simone seriously. "It is now three days since we promenaded, and elles s'ennuyent."

46

"Well, I wish the snow would stop and they could have a good run. As far as that goes, I wouldn't mind one myself," acknowledged Jo.

"But this is not telling us what they did last night," wailed Frieda. "Do tell us, Jo!"

Jo leaned back in her chair, crossed her knees, and prepared to tell the story in full. "Well, you know that silly trick of Evvy's last term—balancing a full inkwell on the end of her ruler without upsetting it?" They all nodded. There had been trouble over that until it had been forbidden by the authorities. "Well, Corney was moved to try to balance it on her head, if you please! I never noticed her, of course—I should jolly soon have put a stop to it if I had. But Maria Marani was in difficulties over her English parsing, and I was trying to find out for her—I was none too sure myself!—just what part of speech "on" was in the sentence, when there was a terrific crash on the floor, and Corney's clarion tones announced, 'Jumping Jehoshaphat! That's done it!' I looked up, and I don't mind owning that I was so floored for a moment I simply said nothing. Corney was sitting there, looking scared for once, and down her face trickled a long stream of school ink. It was running down her nose, and dropping off the end, and the silly little idiot wasn't even *trying* to stop the mess! When I did recover my breath, I made a leap for her, of course, and mopped her up; but her frock was a sight, and it must have gone right through to her undies, for Matey was at me to-day."

"Oh, why?" asked Frieda.

Jo flushed darkly. "Wanted to know what I was doing to let Corney make such a mess of herself during prep. If *she* had to try to keep that room in order and give them any help they needed with their work, she'd soon find it wasn't such an easy matter!"

"And what did the others do?" asked Simone.

"Well, they giggled, of course. I soon shut them up, though."

"And was *that* all?" asked Carla.

47

"No fear! Oh, it was all in the way of that sort of thing. But they whispered and giggled, and I'm almost positive some of them were passing notes, though I couldn't catch them at it."

The Sixth Form looked grave at this. Passing notes was "not done" at the Chalet School. The girls fully recognised that it was thoroughly underhand and deceitful. If they felt they *must* communicate with each other they whispered, and risked being caught and punished. But notes were against the unwritten law.

"We have had no trouble of that kind for more than four years," said Frieda at length. "I do trust it is not going to come now."

"We must all be on our guard when we take prep," said Simone soberly.

"Who is it?" asked Carla.

Joey shook her head. "I couldn't tell you. I only suspect, and I haven't any proof, so it wouldn't be fair to say."

"I do not like it," said Simone. "This means not trusting them, and I do not like that."

"Have you any idea *why* they should write notes?" asked Frieda.

"No; none at all."

The Sixth looked glum. They were quite prepared to deal with mischief; but underhand practices were something they rarely came up against.

They were still sitting thinking, when the door opened, and Marie von Eschenau came in. "Why, how grave you all look!" she exclaimed. "What is wrong?"

"Jo thinks the Middles are passing notes," said Anne Seymour.

"Which Middles?" demanded Marie.

"Oh, some of the Lower Fifth, if it's anyone," said Jo. "But I've nothing to go on really, Marie, so it's no use giving names."

Marie's face registered horror. "Jo! You cannot mean Thekla?"

Jo grinned. "No; I don't. So don't get excited. Even if she did, *you* aren't accountable for your cousin's idiosyncrasies, my dear."

"You never know," said Marie despairingly. "Thekla is Prussian, and she is so strange. She does not at all seem to mind things we dislike!"

"Oh, she's better than she was last term," said Jo.

"It is very little better. I wish Cousin Wolfram had never sent her here."

Jo strolled over, and sat on the arm of the chair into which Marie had collapsed. "Marie, I'm going to say to you something my sister said to me when we had that awful Matron here—during Elisaveta's first term. Do you remember?"

A gleam of mirth lit up Marie's face. "Indeed I do! I remember climbing out of bed and over the verandah to attach snails to her window."

Jo chuckled. "*And* she came bursting out of her room in the middle of the night, with her hair in curling-pins, and said her room was haunted! It must have been fairly ghastly when those snails got going," she added pensively.

Everyone present knew the story, those who had not been at school at the time having heard it from the others. Everyone laughed over the recollection. Jo sobered first.

"I hated Matron, you know," she said casually. "I said so to my sister, and she said to me then that it was all very well being decent when things were smooth; but we often had rough times given us to show what we were. And she said that we'd had a fairly smooth time up till then, and she thought perhaps we needed that experience. Perhaps *we* needed this one now to prove what sort of prefects we really are. Of course, I know we have had any amount of monkey-tricks to settle; but we've never had to meet any thing you could call *nasty*. Perhaps we are to have it now. If we are, it's up to us to show how we can deal with it. And we shan't do that by wailing over it."

"Then what do you advise us to do?" asked Frieda anxiously.

"Just keep your eyes open. If you do catch anyone passing notes, report her to the prefects as a body at once, and we'll deal with it."

That was as far as they could get then, and they began to talk of other things. But every prefect there felt apprehensive about what was coming.

Nothing happened for a few days. Either the need for notes had gone; or else those concerned had taken alarm, and were waiting until the prefects should be lulled into security. The first alarm came from Simone Lecoutier, a full ten days after the prefects had had their conclave.

Joey Bettany, coming up to the prefects' room from a coaching in mediaeval French with jolly little Mademoiselle Lachenais, was confronted by a very angry Simone, who looked, with her flashing eyes and pinched lips, as Jo had never seen Simone before.

"Simone! What on earth is the matter?" she demanded.

"I have a report to make to you as head-girl," said Simone formally.

"What is it?" asked Jo, dropping her books on the table, and facing her chum steadily.

"It is that Kitty Burnett and the new girl, Joyce Linton, and Thekla von Stift have been passing notes," replied Simone. "When I spoke to them about it, they were impudent to me—at least Joyce and Thekla were. They told me to mind my own business; and Thekla added something rude about my countrymen."

"Oh, *hang*!" said Jo aggrievedly. "I do think Thekla might try to behave herself! After all, she *is* Marie's cousin, and it's hard lines on Marie.—Well; what did you do?"

"I told them that I should report them," said Simone. "And Joyce—"

"Well, what did she say?" demanded Joey.

"She said, 'Report if you like—sneak!'" repeated Simone, going suddenly red.

"I hope you didn't rise?" said Jo anxiously. "You didn't answer her, did you, Simone?"

50

She had reason for her anxiety. Simone was an emotional girl, and though her years at the Chalet School had taught her many lessons in self-control she could not always be trusted to guard her tongue.

"I simply repeated that I would report them," said the French girl steadily. "I think I was too angry to say anything more, my Jo."

"Good for you!" Jo's face cleared. "Did Kitty say anything?" she added.

"She giggled. I think she felt ashamed," said Simone.

Jo nodded. "Kit knows, of course, that we don't allow that sort of thing. And she knows what Mary would say about it," she added, naming Kitty Burnett's elder sister, who had been head-girl the previous year at the Chalet School. "All right, Simone. I'll call a meeting after Latin to-morrow afternoon, and we can discuss it then. We must have them up before us, of course. We can't allow this sort of thing. But I'd like to have our plans more or less settled before we deal with them."

"What about Marie?" asked Simone anxiously. She was fond of Marie, and knew how upset she would be by her cousin's behaviour."

"She'll have to know; and she'll be upset, naturally. But it can't be helped. As I said before, no one holds her responsible for her cousin's idiotic behaviour, whatever she may think about it. Have you any idea who began it?"

Simone nodded. "Yes; it is that new child. I do not like her, my Jo. She is not nice. Her sister Gillian I like; but Joyce is enfant gâtée, and she is not sincere."

"Who cheeked you first?" asked Jo.

"Joyce did. But Thekla was not far behind."

"Oh, *drat* the pair of them!" exclaimed Jo fervently—and thereby incurred a reprimand for using improper language from Miss Stewart, the history mistress, who came into the room at that moment in search of some exercise-books which should have been given to her before, and got the full beauty of Jo's invective.

The sharp rebuke for her language silenced Jo for the time being; but when the prefects met in solemn conclave the next day, she had recovered herself, and was able to discuss the affair to the fullest extent.

The prefects were rather nonplussed as to what to do. The impertinence would be dealt with in the usual way. But the dishonesty of note-passing was something fresh.

"We can easily settle Kitty," said Jo shrewdly. "But Thekla and Joyce are a very different matter. We must see that they never sit together again, of course. But I don't know what else we can do."

"I'll tell you," said Frieda Mensch. "We will say that Joyce must do preparation with the Juniors, and Thekla shall do her work with the Upper Fifth and the Sixth."

"It will do for Thekla," said Jo. "I'm afraid we'll have to call it off with Joyce and the Juniors. She couldn't go across to Le Petit Chalet at night—not as long as this weather lasts, anyway." And she glanced out of the window at the snow that was dancing down in dizzying circles.

"Then could we not say they must both work with the Seniors?" suggested Carla. "They will find no one there who would help them to pass notes. And if we warn Anne, she will see that they sit far apart."

"Very well," said Jo. "And I shall make them understand that it is a disgrace, and that we don't trust them. Meeting at half-past sixteen here, you people—Bianca," she turned to a quiet Italian girl, "will you see that they are here then?"

"If I can," said Bianca cautiously. "But what if they refuse to come?"

"Thekla may—Joyce won't," said Jo. "She'll be anxious to know what we're going to do about it. And Kit won't dare to do anything but come."

So it was left, and at the appointed time the prefects sat in dignity round three sides of the table, the fourth being left for the three culprits, who presently came, escorted by Bianca. Kitty had been crying—that was quite plain to be seen. Her blue eyes were swollen, and her rosy cheeks all stained with tears. When she was set opposite a very judicial-looking Jo, she began again, despite a surreptitious kick on the ankle from Joyce, who stood erect, her head well back, her whole attitude showing defiance. Thekla was disdainful, her usual method of meeting English customs she despised—and they were many.

Once the three were there, Jo began at once. "You three have been caught passing notes," she said in chilly tones. "What have you to say for yourselves?"

Kitty sobbed loudly at this, and Jo cast her such a look, that she shivered. "I'm not surprised you cry like that," said the head-girl. "Indeed, after *this*, I don't think anything *you* do could surprise me!"

Joyce sprang to Kitty's defence. "It's all very well for you, Jo Bettany!" she cried. "You can sit there and say horrid things. But if Kitty answers you, you'll say it's cheek and haul her over the coals for *that*! I don't know why you're making all this fuss about a silly little note or two, I'm sure. Everyone does it!"

"Not here," Jo assured her grimly. "Here, we have always considered it utterly dishonourable. Of course, we aren't responsible for the way they thought at your last school."

Joyce flushed. "It was a jolly sight decenter school than this!" she retorted.

"That will do!" said Jo sternly. "You aren't here to be impertinent. Remember that."

Conversation languished for a minute or two after that. Then Thekla spoke in her scornful voice. "I agree with Joyce that this is most unnecessary," she said. "After all, what is there in it that you should make so much fuss, and speak so of dishonour?"

"Why didn't you whisper your messages if they were so important?" demanded Jo.

"And have the mistresses catch us and stop us going to Saturday-night!" said Joyce. "What do you take us for?"

"Well, I *had* hoped you weren't deceitful and underhand," replied Jo thoughtfully. "However, that seems to have been a little mistake on my part."

Even Joyce winced at this, and Kitty sobbed again. Only Thekla was still. Jo proceeded to improve the occasion.

"The fact that you were afraid of losing your Saturday-night if you were caught whispering, and so wrote notes to escape that, only shows us that you knew all the time how mean you were being," she said. "I don't know if any of you realise that you were *stealing* when you did it. Oh, yes you were!"—as Joyce opened her mouth to rebut this—"You were stealing the confidence of the prefect in charge at the time. And you were trading on the fact that the School as a whole considered that sort of thing as dishonest as taking someone else's pocket-money. There is some excuse for Thekla—she hasn't been trained to look at things in the same light as we do. There may be some for Joyce—I don't know about that. Though I must say," she added, "I never imagined that an English high school would have such a poor standard. But there isn't the slightest excuse for Kitty."

"I'm s-s-sorry!" sobbed Kitty. "I ne-never meant to b-be dishonest!"

"If you'd stopped to think for one second, you'd have *known* it was," said Jo relentlessly. "I've got nothing more to say to you. I'm too disgusted with your behaviour. You make me feel sick! Please go away, and don't let us see anything more of you this week if it can be helped. You are a disgrace to the School, and the sooner you realise it the better for you. Now go!"

Crying as if her heart would break, Kitty crept from the room, and sought refuge in her cloakroom, where she cried herself nearly sick. Jo's words had brought home to her just what she had done; and the knowledge that her own greatly admired elder sister would have been even sterner when she was head-girl made everything seem much worse. Kitty Burnett was heedless, but she was not dishonourable, and the head-girl's sweeping condemnation of her behaviour gave her a check which made her less thoughtless for the rest of her life.

Kitty having been disposed of, Jo proceeded to deal with the other two.

"Thekla, you are the oldest," she said. "However, as I said before, I don't think you realise yet what we think about such things. Perhaps after another term or two you'll have managed to take it in. As it is, you can miss the next two Saturdays. You can go to Matron about it, but I expect it will mean early bed.—As for you, Joyce, you seem to be somewhat above yourself, and the only thing I can suggest is that you should try to realise that you are only a Middle—and a very new Middle at that. It's rather too early for you to have assimilated our ideals, I suppose, though your sister doesn't seem to have had such trouble. Just get it into your head that all such things as passing notes are despised here, and the people who do them are considered despicable. And remember that you are really a very insignificant person, as well. You can take the same punishment as Thekla, and I hope it'll teach you not to indulge in such practices. Now you may go—unless anyone else would like to say anything to either of you." She looked inquiringly round the ranks of the prefects, but they all shook their heads. They felt that Jo had handled the situation very thoroughly—too thoroughly, almost, one or two of them thought. Judging by the expression on Joyce's face, it would be long before she forgave the head-girl all the hurts her pride had just received.

Seeing nothing else for it, Thekla led the way out of the room, and Joyce followed her, inwardly raging. That *she*, Joyce Linton, should be spoken to like that! It was outrageous! When they were outside, she swung round, and fled to her dormitory, where she shed tears almost as bitter as poor Kitty, until Matron, coming in for some reason, caught her there, and after scolding her sharply for breaking rules, sent her to the bathroom to wash her face before going downstairs to give in the order-mark she had just been awarded.

CHAPTER VI

THE MIDNIGHT FEAST

Jo's drastic treatment of the "notes" episode put a stop to that particular form of ill-doing. But Joyce didn't forget, and she made up her mind to "get square" somehow. For one thing, Gillian had heard of it, and she had reproached her young sister for her share in the matter, till Joyce suddenly flared up, and crying, "Oh, mind your own business, and leave me to mind mine!" rushed off.

Naturally Jo had nothing to do with Gillian's share in the matter, but Joyce chose to blame her for it, and considered that she was a most ill-used person. The friends she had made were of little help to her, for they were, for the most part, heedless young persons, who were under the thrall of her prettiness and the charming manners she could show on occasion, and were not likely to attempt to restrain her in any way.

Joyce brooded over her wrongs for a whole week, at the end of which time she had thought of something to do. She had made cautious inquiries of the others, and found that though the Chalet Middles possessed a reputation for mischief that could certainly not have been bettered anywhere, they had never indulged in a midnight feast.

"Oh, why not?" cried Joyce when she heard this. "I've always thought that would be one of the best things about boarding-school!"

"I suppose it is that we always have plenty, and it is so delicious," said Hilda Bhaer, the person to whom she was speaking.

"Oh, but that hasn't anything to do with it!" said Joyce quickly. "It's the fun of having it when everyone's in bed, and the risk of being caught, and all that sort of thing."

But Hilda was not adventurous. "I think it would be very cold," she said with a slight shiver.

Joyce glanced out of the window where the snow was falling with a vim that seemed to say it would be many a long hour before it stopped. "Of course we'd have to wrap up," she agreed. "If we all caught colds and started 'flu it wouldn't be much fun."

"English, Joyce? Have you forgotten that this is German day?" asked Frieda Mensch, who came past in time to hear Joyce's last remark. "A fine, please, and don't forget again."

She went on, and Joyce stamped her foot. "What a sickening nuisance those prees are!" she said fervently. "I loathe the lot of them!"

"That is because you get into so much trouble with them," said Hilda, who was not a tactful young person. "Try to remember, Joyce, for it is the rule, and indeed we must keep it."

"Oh, hang! Do stop talking like a goody-good book!" retorted Joyce.

As she still spoke in English, she fully deserved to be caught again, but for once Fate was kind to her; and gentle, phlegmatic Hilda rarely took offence.

Joyce went off to put her fine into the box, wishing as she went that they had never come here; and Hilda departed to seek Rosa van Buren, who had borrowed her Latin grammar and not returned it.

Whether it was Frieda's punishment, or whether it was her natural love of adventure, Joyce made up her mind to hold that "midnight" by hook or crook. She selected with care those who were to participate, for already she knew that a good many of the girls would frown on it. This also meant that it could not be held in the dormitory. But Joyce had pitched on a small room near the head of the stairs, which was used by Matron for a sewing-room. It was at the other end of the corridor from that lady's own bedroom, and that was an advantage. Matey was popularly reported to have the hearing of a lynx!

It was not so hard to get food, for a fine day came, and the girls were all bundled up, and escorted to Spärtz, the little market-town at the foot of the mountain, so that they might have a thorough change. They were allowed to divide up into parties, each party having a mistress or a prefect in charge, and they went to the shops to do the small errands they all had.

Joyce, after some thought, attached herself to Vanna di Ricci, one of the less prominent prefects, and taking advantage of the fact that Vanna went into the biggest shop in the little town on a quest for "animal" biscuits for Jo Bettany to take up to the Sonnalpe for her nephews and niece the next time she went, contrived to invest in sardines, apricot jam, sugar-biscuits, and a tin of condensed milk. She was forced to borrow from Gillian to pay for them, most of her pocket-money having gone in fines, but Gillian was so glad to see her interested and happy, she would have willingly stripped herself of every penny.

The rest of the party also managed to add to the commissariat, and if their purchases were strikingly varied, that, as Joyce said later on, only added to the interest of the feast. They all had big pockets in their coats, and as they all wore their shawls crossed over and tied behind, it was easily to slip such contraband as sardines and condensed milk into the folds where they were less likely to be noticed.

The feast itself was to take place next day, which was Saturday. If it was a fine day Jo Bettany and Frieda Mensch were to go up to the Sonnalpe to spend the week-end with their respective sisters, and Gillian would also go, to see her mother, and stay at "Die Rosen" again, while Elsie Carr, a pretty, dark-haired girl of fifteen, with whom Gillian had struck up quite a friendship, would join them, for she had an elder sister in the Sanatorium, though, as the whole School knew, Lilias Carr was cured

58

now, and was only remaining on in the Tyrol till the summer as an extra precaution.

With two of the principal prefects and her own elder sister away, Joyce felt that there might be some chance of carrying out her plan safely. The others agreed with her, and so it was arranged.

There was a little cupboard in the sewing-room, where oddments were kept, and here the girls contrived to deposit most of their stock before the evening. And a queer mixture it was, for every girl had satisfied her own taste in food. Joyce surveyed the packages happily when she contrived to slip in during the afternoon. At least they would have *enough*!

"I got sardines, so we'd better take up some bread to eat with them," she informed her band just before Kaffee und Kuchen.

"We can't all do it," protested Enid Sothern, a pickle of about twelve years old, and a devoted follower of the new girl.

"Oh, well, we older ones will, then," said Joyce, rather too vaguely, as it turned out later.

It was left at that, and the party dispersed—just in time, too, for Marie von Eschenau came downstairs the next minute, and she would certainly have wondered what seven Middles were doing on the stairs just then. The snow, which had cleared off during the night, had begun falling again shortly after midday, so though they had had a jolly romp outside in the morning, there had been no hope of another, and after Mittagessen—or dinner—they had all settled down in the form-rooms and the common-room with books and table games.

Thekla von Stift had not been with them. She was indolent by nature, and preferred the warmth of the common-room and her comfortable basket-chair near the stove to parading up to the sewing-room. She had given her contribution to Luise Rotheim, the only other member of the Lower Fifth, Hilda Bhaer, and Joyce to be among the malcontents, and Luise had conveyed it to the cupboard when she had taken her own. The other members of the party were Klara Melnarti, a chum of Enid Sothern's, and second only to her in mischief; Margritta Ajockz, another member of the Fourth Form; and Mary Shaw from the Third, where she was ringleader. They had rather kicked against having Mary, but she had been with their shopping party, and had become curious when Klara bought a tin of spaghetti. She had worried Klara until that young lady had given away the secret, whereupon Mary insisted on being allowed to join. They had reluctantly agreed on her promising not to let the rest know, so she had trotted along with her contribution to the feast, and was hugging herself that she was "in with the big girls."

"How do we arrange?" asked Klara with a giggle when they were all safely in the Fifth form-room again, where there was nobody but themselves.

"Wait until you hear eleven o'clock strike," began Joyce.

"Eleven—wie—I do not understand," put in Margritta with a puzzled look.

"Oh—bother!" Joyce proceeded to count up hastily on her fingers. "Twenty-three, then. When you do hear it, get up and put on your dressing-gown, and come along as quietly as you can. For goodness' sake don't wake up any of the others in your dormy, Margritta!"

"No, I will not," promised Margritta.

"And don't undress properly, either. It'll be jolly cold if you do, and if we all have snuffles next day, Matey's sure to guess something's been up—she's got such a nasty, suspicious mind!"

Then the bell rang for Kaffee und Kuchen, and they all went back to the common-room, looking as though butter wouldn't melt in their mouths. If Jo had been about, she would certainly have suspected something. But Jo was at the Sonnalpe, having a good time with her nephews and niece and the Robin, and knew nothing about it. The rest of the prefects were not so ready to see things, though

60

Simone Lecoutier did ask Marie if she thought any of that particular crowd could be ill, they were so little trouble.

"Oh, I expect they are tired with the snowballing this morning," said Marie happily. "Do not worry, Simone. We dance to-night, so they can get into no mischief."

With this, Simone was fain to be satisfied, and as Vanna di Ricci called her attention to something the next moment, she forgot all about it.

How the eight wished the evening would come to an end, I leave anyone interested in this story to guess. It seemed to them as if they had been dancing for hours when the bell rang for Prayers, and they parted—the Catholics to the Fourth form-room, and the Protestants to stay where they were. Then came bedtime, and Joyce, for one, began to wonder if lights-out would never sound. But at last Simone who was on duty rang the bell, and then Bianca di Ferrara, the prefect for their corridor, came to switch off the light, and bid them good-night.

After that, there was a long period, and then Joyce, lying awake in her bed, heard subdued voices on the stairs which told her that such of the Staff as lived in the Chalet were coming to bed too. She felt under her pillow for her watch and torch, and anxiously looked at the time. Half-past ten! How fearfully late the Staff were to-night! They ought to go to bed at *least* half an hour before this!

However, the Staff were evidently tired, for soon all sounds ceased, and when Joyce ventured to get up and steal down the aisle between the cubicles of her dormitory, she couldn't hear a sound. Neither was there any light to be seen with the exception of the very dim light of the night-bulb which burned in every corridor all night.

She slipped quietly along to the sewing-room, and went in. It was in darkness, but she had her own torch, and she had "borrowed" Gillian's as well, so that when Enid Sothern, the next to arrive, came in with *her* torch, there was a dim light in the room. Hilda Bhaer was the only one of the party who had not arrived, and Joyce was just

61

debating whether she should risk going to wake her when Hilda came, very much ashamed of herself, for she had fallen asleep, and had awakened with a start at ten minutes past eleven—or twenty-three, as all the girls called it.

"We must have thought-transferred you," said Joyce with a giggle as she shut the door softly after the late-comer. "That's what woke you, I expect."

"Or else the cold," said Thekla with a shiver. "If I had known how cold it is, I would never have left my warm bed."

"Oh, rats!" said Joyce lightly. "It's not too bad. After all, the place is centrally heated. You aren't half a sport, Thekla, if you're going to mind a little coolness. Now then, come on and get out the eats!"

The girls hastened to the cupboard, and while Joyce and Luise handed out the food, the rest set it out on the clean bureau-cover that Joyce had brought from her cubicle. It looked a fine selection when it was all there, though Joyce, Enid, and Mary were rather startled at some of the things. Most of the girls had bought sausages. There were one or two tins of fruit and Joyce's tins of sardines. Klara, who had had a hamper from home that morning, donated a huge cake that was black with richness; and Margritta had bought oranges and bananas. For drink, they would have chocolate made with hot water (from the thermos flasks of those that had them) and a cake of chocolate which Luise Rotheim produced. Joyce's tinned milk would have to sweeten it, as no one had thought of bringing sugar. Then Joyce, with rather the air of a conjuror, produced a tin-opener which she had procured from the kitchen earlier in the day—by what means, she alone knew—and they decided to begin with the sardines. Joyce opened them carefully, for they dared not spill any oil—that would have been a certain way to bring down discovery on themselves.

"Now then, hand out the bread and butter," she said cheerfully when she had finished.

There was a silence. Everyone looked blankly at everyone else.

"Come on—hurry up!" said Joyce impatiently. Then she looked up. "Do you mean to say none of you remembered it?" she demanded.

"But you said the elder ones would get it," protested Mary. "Guess I never thought of it again. *Say!* Have we to eat 'em in our fingers? What a mess we'll be in!" And she giggled infectiously.

Joyce looked disgusted. "No; of course not! We'd make ourselves so oily and then the towels would show, and Matey would guess. Oh, I do think some of you might have remembered! I did tell you!"

Eventually, it was decided that the best way was to cut slices off Klara's cake, and lay the sardines on them. It was done, and they ate the queer mixture—Joyce not without some misgivings. She knew that she was rather easily upset.

The fruit was handed round, and they ate *that* in their fingers, taking it in turns to drink the syrup out of the tins. Their thermos flasks must be left for the chocolate which Luise compounded. It was hot, but it had a queer flavour, and one or two of them felt inclined to cavil at the lack of sugar. Still, they all declared they enjoyed it. The oranges and bananas followed—they had eaten the sausages after the sardines—and they wound up with sweets, which were Mary Shaw's donation. Finally, there was nothing left but a parcel Thekla had. She opened it, and displayed to view rashers of raw bacon!

"*Thekla!*" gasped Joyce when she had recovered from the shock. "Whatever possessed you to get *that*? We can't possibly cook it! It would smell all over the place!"

"But there is no need to cook it," said Thekla calmly. "It is smoked—see!" And she held it so that they saw that the rind was a rich red-brown.

"But you can't eat it *raw*!" exclaimed Enid.

"Why not?" demanded Thekla, raising brows of haughty query.

63

"Eat raw bacon?"

"Certainly! I have told you it is smoked.—Luise, will you have some?"

Luise shook her head and giggled. "I am so—what do you say?—so full, I could not hold one thing more."

Joyce, Enid, and Mary all refused the delicacy; and Klara announced that *she* felt sick, and couldn't touch it. It was left to Thekla to enjoy it alone, and she ate a whole rasher, though Joyce turned her eyes away, for, like Klara, she was feeling poorly, and she knew that if she saw Thekla eating the uncooked stuff, it would finish her. Finally, they gathered up the crumbs, and put them into the empty stove. The tins were pushed to the back of the cupboard, for they had no other means of disposing of them. Klara took up the remains of her cake; and Margritta tucked the orange and banana skins into the pocket of her dressing-gown. When everything looked as tidy as they could make it, they all whispered that they had had a delightful time, and had enjoyed themselves very much. Then they parted, and went off to their dormitories. For once, Fate was kind to delinquents, and they got back to bed in safety. Joyce, laying her weary head on her pillow, thought that they had managed very well. No one would find out, for it was unlikely that the tins would be discovered on the morrow, and some of them ought to be able to get them safely away before Monday.

Then she cuddled down under her plumeau, and tried to go to sleep.

CHAPTER VII

NEMESIS

CORNELIA FLOWER, head of the Violet dormitory by right of age, was fast asleep, and dreaming wildly that she was crossing the Atlantic on a raft. It was a terribly rough passage, and the raft kept going up and down so violently that Cornelia made up her mind that she would shortly be seasick. "There must be a *sea*quake going on," she said to herself. "Nothing else could make it as rough as all this. Guess the sooner I get across the better."

At this point she came back to consciousness, and the realisation that someone was shaking her vehemently, and crying, "Corney—*Corney*! Oh, do wake up! Joyce is ever so ill, and I don't know what to do!"

With a gasp, Cornelia sat up in bed and opened her eyes—only to close them again for a moment, for a brilliant light was glaring straight into them. At the same time, she heard little, heart-rending moans coming from somewhere close at hand. She opened her eyes cautiously again, and found that Violet Allison and Greta Macdonald, two of the girls in the dormitory, were standing by her bedside. Violet had been doing the shaking, and it was Greta who was holding the light which had dazzled her.

"Hello!" she said. "What's wrong?"

"It's Joyce," said Violet with a little shiver, for the night was cold, and she had forgotten to put on either dressing-gown or bedroom slippers. "She's dreadfully ill, Corney. What shall we do?"

"Go back and put on your dressing-gown, you—idiot," said Corney, restraining her tongue in time. She possessed a wide vocabulary of epithets mostly forbidden at school, and it was not always easy to remember what she might use and what she mightn't.

By this time, she had fully awakened, and the sounds that were coming from Joyce's corner of the room rather frightened her. But Cornelia was fifteen now, and the other children were only thirteen, so she knew she must keep her head. She got up, and flung on her own dressing-gown, and stuck her feet into her slippers. Then she paddled across the room to Joyce's cubicle, and pulled back the curtains. "Go and switch on the light, Greta," she said, as she bent over the younger girl. "You can't see a mite with that torch."

Greta did as she was asked, and then she, and Violet, now properly arrayed, çame back to the cubicle where Cornelia was asking Joyce what was wrong.

"Are you sick?" asked the American girl, using the term in the American sense.

Joyce moaned. "*Sick!* I never felt so awful in my life!"

"Here, Vi! You scoot and fetch Matey," ordered Cornelia. She felt rather alarmed, for Joyce was a queer whitish-green in hue, and her hands felt so cold and clammy when the elder girl touched them. "And Greta, you'd better hop back to bed. There'll only be a fuss if we're all here when Matey comes."

"Can't I help at all?" asked Greta. "Shall I bring my bottle?"

"Yes; and mine, too," said Cornelia. "She's like a lump of ice!"

The two hot-water bottles were brought, and one was tucked in at Joyce's feet, and the other shoved down behind her back. Then Cornelia, clutching at her sick-nurse training, sent Greta to the bathroom to see if the water in the taps was hot, and if so, to bring a glassful. The water proved to be fairly hot, and Greta brought the glass. Cornelia slipped an arm under Joyce's head, and held the glass to her lips.

"No—no!" moaned the patient.

"Guess you'd better," said Cornelia persuasively. "Come

66

on, Joycie! Just a sip! It's only hot water, and it'll maybe warm you a mite."

Thus urged, Joyce tried to sit up, and thereby wrought her own undoing. By the time Matron came from the upper dormitory, whither Violet had had to follow her, Joyce was thoroughly and completely sick. Cornelia had kept her head, and sent Greta for a basin from the bathroom, but she was unfeignedly thankful to have someone in authority to take charge. She felt that things were getting beyond her.

Matron had a stiff time of it. Joyce was really ill, as the result of the appalling mixture she had swallowed, and it was a good hour before they were able to roll her in blankets and carry her along to San. Matron had sent Cornelia for Miss Annersley, the senior mistress, and Miss Annersley in her turn roused Moida, one of the maids, to light the kitchen stove and heat water for bottles.

"I can't understand it!" said Matron anxiously, as she mixed sal-volatile for Joyce. "She's had nothing that could have upset her like this, and yet she is really ill."

"A chill, perhaps?" suggested Miss Annersley, who was holding the half-fainting child up in her arms. "There, Joyce! You'll be all right soon."

After another violent spasm of sickness, Matron dosed her with sal-volatile, and then settled down to watch its effects. "If this doesn't check it, I must try brandy," she said. "I don't like giving it to children, but we must stop this sickness somehow."

"Shall I ring up Dr. Erckhardt?" asked Miss Annersley. "It would be easier for him to get up than for the Sonnalpe people to get down. Besides, they are all very busy up there, I know. Mrs. Russell told me that they have some very bad cases, and they are all working to the limit."

Matron shook her head. "Not yet, I think. I don't believe it's anything more than an extra-violent bilious attack. She was certainly all right when she went to bed, and no illness could develop with quite such rapidity."

Luckily, her remedies began to take effect shortly after, and by six o'clock in the morning Joyce was lying, very limp and pallid, but feeling more like herself.

And then Sophie Hamel, the prefect who was head of the Green dormitory, came along to report that Mary Shaw had been sick, and complained of pain.

"*What?*" Matron was galvanised into an upright position, though a moment before she had been bending over Joyce, who seemed inclined to doze a little.

"She has been very sick, Matron," said Sophie. "I gave her hot water to drink, and rolled her in a blanket, but she cries very much, and says she has pain."

"I'll come.—Miss Annersley, will you stay with Joyce till I return?" And Matron stalked out of the room after Sophie, resolved in her own mind to find out what was at the bottom of all this. When Violet had been hunting for her, she had been with Thekla von Stift, who had roused her whole dormitory by wild nightmare from which they were unable to wake her. Matron had wakened her, needless to state, and she had meant to go back later on to see how the girl was sleeping. But Joyce's attack had seemed so serious, that she had had no time. And now, here was Mary Shaw also bilious, judging by Sophie's account. There was something behind it all, for Matron knew that the food they had had the day before would not account for all this.

She found Mary very poorly and inclined to be desperately sorry for herself, but not nearly so ill as Joyce. She had wakened very sick, and she had the pain her orgy merited; but already the effects were passing off. Matron bundled her up in a blanket, and took her to the school Sanatorium, where she tucked her into bed with a couple of hot bottles, gave her some sal-volatile, and soon had the satisfaction of seeing her drop off to sleep.

But Joyce roused up, complaining of fresh sickness, and from then until midday she had recurring bouts, till Matron was thankful to see Dr. Erckhardt from Spärtz, when he strode into the room. Mary was better, and was back in her own dormitory, feeling very sorry for herself, and very hollow. But Joyce was completely exhausted by the sickness, and she lay limply on her pillows, every scrap of her pretty colour gone; her very curls dank and straight on her brows.

"They have eaten something to disagree with them," was the doctor's verdict when he had heard Matron's account and examined his patients. "That is it without a doubt. The little one has not been seized so badly; but this one has had a severe attack."

"Then it's something they've had apart from the school meals," said Matron with decision. "I shall have to find out what it is later on. An older girl disturbed another dormitory through having nightmare last night, and I feel pretty sure that it is all from the one cause."

The doctor nodded. "Perhaps they have been eating too many sweets and cakes. However, castor-oil will soon put them all right again, and, doubtless be a lesson to them not to be greedy another time."

He departed after that, and Matron set to work and mixed three jorums of castor-oil. Then she went to the Green dormitory where Mary was lying, feeling somewhat ashamed now that she was better, and wishing that she might get up, for it was very dull lying in bed with nothing to do.

"Now, then," said Matron briskly, "sit up and take this. Then, if you are all right, you may, perhaps, get up for an hour or so this afternoon. There isn't much wrong with you now."

Mary sat up obediently; but when she took the cup and saw what it contained, her face lengthened woefully. "Oh, Matron! It's such a lot!" she protested.

"And girls who disturb everyone else during the night because they have been greedy require a good dose," retorted Matron grimly. "Down with it, and don't keep me standing here when I'm nearly run off my feet as it is!"

With Matron looking and sounding like that, Mary saw

no help for it. She shut her eyes, swallowed the nauseous draught as best she could, and then collapsed shuddering on her pillows. "Oooh! What *horrid* stuff it is!"

Matron produced a piece of dry bread. "Eat that, and the taste will go," she ordered.

Mary obeyed meekly, and then lay down again, resolving in her own mind never to have anything to do with a midnight feast again. Matron covered her up, after feeling her hot bottle to be sure that it was still comfortably warm, and then departed to dose Joyce.

Joyce was still too limp and weak to rebel. She took the oil without a word, and Matron, after settling her, sent Violet Allison, who was passing at the time, to tell Thekla von Stift to come to her room.

Thekla, who had already had a fierce battle with Luise Rotheim that morning over whether they should confess or not, started guiltily when she heard Violet's message. She would have liked to refuse, but "Matey" was not a person you could disobey with impunity, so she went upstairs reluctantly.

"Violet says you wish to see me, Matron," she said stiffly in her own tongue.

"So I do," said Matron vigorously. "You had nightmare last night, so you must have been eating something to disagree with you. Can't have that sort of thing going on, so you'll have to have some medicine to set you right. Here you are—drink it up."

Thekla took the cup and looked at its contents. Then she set it down on the table. "I am quite well, and I do not need this," she said.

"Nonsense! You don't get nightmare for nothing!" said Matron brusquely. "Take it at once, Thekla, and let me have no more nonsense!"

Thekla set her lips. "I will not drink this," she said. "I am quite well and do not need it. Besides, I dislike it."

"So do most folk," said Matron. "That doesn't alter the case, however. Either you drink this without any

70

trouble; or I'll treat you as if you were one of the Juniors, and hold your nose. But drink it you shall."

Matron was not tall, but she was very wiry, and there was no doubt that she was perfectly capable of doing as she said. Thekla hated castor-oil, but she had no mind to be treated like a baby. She took the cup again, and after one or two efforts, contrived to down its contents.

"Now you may go," said the tyrant of the San. "I'll see you this evening before Abendessen, and then you can explain to me just why you three have been upset like this."

Dreadfully uncomfortable in her mind, Thekla left the room. She didn't want to say anything about the night before, for she guessed that there would be trouble over it. She was the oldest girl who had been present, though Luise was only a few months younger. She had the feeling that she would receive a good share of the blame, and she felt that she didn't deserve it. If Joyce Linton hadn't suggested it, she would never have thought of doing such a thing.

As it happened, there was no need for Matron to see Thekla. Luise Rotheim, urged thereto by a most uneasy conscience, had sought out Miss Annersley at the time that the castor-oil controversy was going on in Matron's room, and was confessing everything to her, as Mademoiselle Lepâttre was up at the Sonnalpe for the weekend on business concerns.

To say that Miss Annersley was startled, is to express it mildly.

"You mean to say that eight of you went to the little sewing-room and had a feast?" she exclaimed. "*When* did you go?"

"At half-past twenty-three," faltered Luise.

"Where did you get the food?"

Luise told her, and Miss Annersley's expression became more and more grim as the girl stumbled on.

"I suppose you were not alone—you, and Joyce, and Mary, and Thekla—Oh, but you said eight of you. Go and tell the others to come to me here at once, and come back yourself. Not Joyce or Mary, of course. They are still in bed, and Joyce has been very ill indeed. But the rest."

Luise went, now thoroughly miserable, and presently returned with the others. She and Thekla looked flushed, and Thekla was plainly angry. She had been furious when Luise owned that she had confessed, and if she had dared, she would have refused to come. But there it was. In this wretched place you didn't dare refuse—or at any rate, not for long. As for Hilda, Margritta, Enid, and Klara, they were, in their secret souls, not sorry that it had all come out. They had heard wildly-exaggerated rumours about Joyce Linton's illness, and they knew the cause of it very well. Cornelia Flower had embellished her account of the night's happenings, and Violet and Greta had assured them that they thought Joyce was going to die, she was so ill! So far, Sunday had been a thoroughly miserable day to them, and, as Enid said later on, if they got their share of trouble, it would make them feel better in their minds, anyhow.

Having got the five together, Miss Annersley catechised them severely, till she had got most of the story out of them. Inwardly, she was consumed with admiration for their digestive powers. Outwardly, she was all that convention demanded she should be. She told them that she was bitterly ashamed to think that Chalet girls could be so greedy and thoughtless. She impressed on them the seriousness of Joyce's illness. She added that this meant that they were not to be trusted—which reduced Luise, Hilda, and Margritta to tears at once—and then she issued sentence. For a whole week they would have no cakes, no jam, no sweets, and no fancy-bread. They would be allowed only the simplest and plainest of food. Also, as they obviously did not know how to spend their money wisely, all they had would be confiscated, and it would be doled out to them only for necessary expenses until Half-term, by which time she hoped they would have learned a

72

little more sense. The same punishments would apply to Joyce and Mary when they were better.

"But why should we have no less punishment than Joyce?" cried Thekla. "It was her idea!"

Miss Annersley took no notice of this. As she said later on, if you once listen to tales, you are lost. Besides, she had no great fondness for Thekla von Stift, who had been a tiresome pupil all the previous term, and seemed little improved this. So she merely told the girls they might go, and then went back to her book which had been laid aside when Luise came with her story. Presently she laid it down, and began to laugh. She laughed till the tears ran down her face as she thought of the shock some of the feasters must have got when Thekla insisted on eating her raw bacon.

"But it's just as well Matron gave her a stiff dose of castor-oil," she thought when she was calm once more. "Otherwise, we might have fresh trouble later on. As for Joyce, it strikes me she will bear watching."

And so said the rest of the Staff when they heard what had caused the upset which had worried them all so much.

CHAPTER VIII

STAFF-EVENING

THE people who had been spending the week-end at the Sonnalpe came down on Monday morning to find Joyce still in bed and Mary out of school, as a result of their Saturday-night orgy. The rest of the party were very subdued, even Thekla wearing a depressed air very unlike her. Naturally, the latest was poured into the ears of the four, and they promptly expressed themselves on the subject with point.

"I'm not surprised at *anything* those Middles do!" said Jo. "But I must say I didn't think they could be quite such pigs! As for Hilda and Luise, they ought to be ashamed of themselves. They've been here longer than any of the others, and they know quite well that that sort of thing isn't done."

"Oh, how *could* Joyce?" cried Gillian. "She's awfully easily upset, and what Mummy would think if she knew, I don't know She'd be horribly worried."

"I expect Joyce did not think about that," put in gentle Frieda, always ready to live up to the meaning of her name and to make peace. "Perhaps it was the excitement that attracted her."

"And perhaps it wasn't," said Elsie Carr. "She's your sister, Gill, but I must say I think her behaviour's the limit!—Who else was in it, did you say, Evvy?"

Evadne Lannis, their informant, obliged at once. "Thekla, and Margritta and Enid, and Mary Shaw. Mary was pretty sick yesterday, but she's most fit now, though Matey won't let her come into school till to-morrow. Thekla had nightmare and woke us all up by screeching in the night. We couldn't rouse her, though we sure shook up her brains. The rest don't seem to have hurt any."

"They've got a nice punishment, anyhow," said Anne Seymour, balancing on the back of a chair. "No cakes or sweets for a week; and no pocket-money except for absolute necessities!"

"They jolly well deserve it," said Jo, "and I hope it's taught them a lesson."

However, the Staff-evening, which had been postponed unavoidably till that week, was to take place on the Saturday, so after Monday no one troubled much about the latest affair. It is true that Joyce was furious when she found that it had all been found out, and did not spare her words when she met Luise. But that young lady had been brought to her senses with a sharp jerk, and she refused to regret anything she had done. Finding it no use, Joyce desisted; but she by no means forgot, and she vowed she would "get square" with the Austrian girl before they were much older.

The work that had to be crammed into the last two days of the school week gave her no chance for it then, and Saturday brought with it such a feeling of excitement that she shelved the matter for the time being.

"What do they do with us?" asked Gillian of Evadne Lannis during the mending-hour that morning.

"No idea," said Evadne, who hated sewing of any kind, and was in trouble over a huge hole in her stocking-heel.

"They gave a fancy-dress dance one year," said Carla von Flügen, who happened to be sitting near them. "And another year they left it till the summer term, and we had a picnic up on the Mondscheinspitze."

"And the year before that they had it in the Christmas term, and they dressed up as pierrots and gave us a concert," put in Sophie Hamel.—"Scissors, please, Evvy."

"I can tell you what it *won't* be this year," said Jo, stitching at the finger-ends of her gloves with great rapidity, and more heed for strength than beauty in her sewing. "They haven't had any floors waxed, so it's not going to be a dance."

"Hasn't any one any idea?" asked Gillian plaintively.

"I rather like to know what's coming so that I can be prepared."

"No; but it will be something very pleasant, I know," Marie von Eschenau assured her.—"There! That is the last of my mending! Now I must write to Mamma, for I have not answered her last letter."

"And I must write to Bernhilda," said Frieda, rolling up her last pair of stockings.

"Give her my love," mumbled Jo, who was biting off the end of her thread as she spoke.

"And mine!"—"And mine, too!" The chorus ran quickly round. Frieda's sister had been very popular when she was at the school, and she still held her place in the affections of those girls who had known her.

"There's the bell; and I haven't finished these stockings yet!" groaned Evadne. "I just despise sewing!"

"Give them to me. I will finish them for you," said Marie, stretching out her hand for them.

Evadne shook her head. "Guess I'll do my own dirty work—thanks, all the same. But I sure wish someone would invent stockings that *never* went holey!"

"There's a fortune waiting for the man that *does*!" said Jo feelingly. "To say nothing of the blessings of millions! Come on! We shall be late for Guides if we don't buck up."

They put their sewing away, and then scurried off to Guide meeting which was always held at this hour on Saturdays. Both Gillian and Joyce had been Guides in England, and it had been an easy matter to arrange for their transfers. Matron said she was thankful. Such girls as were not Guides came to her for extra needlework, and one of the Staff took them for a walk at noon if it were fine. Matron was always busy, and she was inclined to resent this taking up of her time.

After Guides, they raced upstairs to change from uniform to the brown velveteen frocks they always wore when not in uniform. No one was going up to the Sonnalpe to-day, for no one wanted to miss the Staff-evening.

76

"What shall we do this afternoon?" asked Gillian as she came downstairs again behind Elsie Carr.

"Walk, of course. It's a jolly day," said Elsie appreciatively. "Just look at the sun! I expect the snow will begin to go presently, so that means an early spring."

"It will be awfully messy when it *does* thaw—all that snow!" said Gillian.

Margia Stevens who was with them laughed. "You haven't been here before or you'd know that it goes like a flash," she said. "We don't have the awful days and days of mud you get in England. We generally have high winds, and they dry it off in half no time."

"Wonder if we'll have a flood this year?" said Cornelia Flower pensively. "Remember last year?"

"I should think I do! That was when poor old Stacie got hurt," replied Elsie.

Gillian had been told the tale of Stacie's accident. She also knew that when the girl had run away, after making herself thoroughly miserable at school by her priggish, silly ways, she had doomed herself to a far worse punishment than anyone had foreseen at the time. But that accident had helped to peel off the veneer which had hidden the real girl from view, and Stacie herself said that in some ways it had been worth it after nearly a whole year of being chained to her couch.

The walk was quite a jolly one, for the day was mild, and the girls had had so much confinement to the house owing to the storms which had come after Christmas, that they were somewhat out of walking trim. They went round the lake to Seehof, far down on the bank opposite to Briesau where the school was situated. Here there was a big hotel which, however, was closed at this season of the year. When they reached it, Miss Wilson, who was in charge, gave the word, and they turned back, for the more open weather had made it dangerous to attempt to cross the lake on the ice. It was quite half an hour past their usual time when they got back for Kaffee und Kuchen, and they ate in considerable excitement.

77

Just as they were finishing, the door of the common-room opened, and Miss Leslie, the mathematics mistress, appeared. "I've just come to tell you people not to change to-night," she announced briskly. "We aren't going to dance, and Mademoiselle thinks you will be warmer in your velveteens."

"Miss Leslie, be a gem and tell us what you are going to do," coaxed Anne Seymour.

Miss Leslie laughed. "What cool impudence! If I did, I should deserve to be—turned out of it altogether! No; you may hold your horses till nineteen this evening, Anne. It's not so very long now." Then she whisked away, and the girls were left to their speculations.

At Abendessen, which came at half-past eighteen that night, a message was brought to Jo to say that the Staff were having their meal by themselves, and the prefects were to take charge in the Speisesaal. When the girls had finished, they were to go to the hall which had been built for such affairs, and take their seats.

"Then it's a play or something like that, and they're all dressed and made up, and don't want us to see them," decided Jo aloud. "What fun! Hurry on, everyone. The sooner we're finished, the sooner to have the fun!"

After that, everyone ate at a rate which would have drawn remonstrances at least from Matron, had she been there to see them. When the meal was over, Jo said grace and then rapped on the table with a fork.

"Anyone who wants to wash fall out and stand by the windows," she ordered. "The rest of you lead on into Hall. Juniors have cushions on the floor, and the rest sit as you like; only no scrums! Marie and Frieda will take charge. Simone and I will look after the folk who want to go to the Splasheries."

They formed into line, and while the majority went into Hall, Jo and Simone led the rest off to the Splasheries to see that people merely washed their hands, and indulged in no wild pranks. Then they, too, went on, and presently the big room was full of girls, all laughing and chattering, and speculating as to what was to come. Some of the girls were in favour of scenes from Shakespeare or Molière. Others thought it must be a modern comedy. Cornelia Flower nearly brought down the house by suggesting that the staff would do "Charley's Aunt"!

"As if they *could*!" scoffed Jo. "Do talk sense, Corney!"

"*I* know," said Frieda, with a wicked look at one or two people near at hand. "They are going to perform some of the Ku Klux Klan scenes out of those 'Elsie' books of Jo's."

The persons hit at went red and wriggled. They themselves had tried to utilise those scenes for their own nefarious purposes. But how mean of Frieda to drag it up after more than a year!

However, the curtains draped across the platform at the top end of the room were being drawn apart, so Evadne, Margia, Cornelia, Cyrilla, and the rest of that coterie held their tongues, and stared eagerly. The next moment the stage was in full view, and the excited girls saw a strange sight.

At one side was a lady who was nearly as broad as she was long. She wore an ample skirt of black, with a huge, Paisley-patterned shawl, a bonnet of the coal-scuttle shape adorned with a perfect flower-garden of artificial flowers. A coal-black corkscrew curl peeped out at either side of a rubicund face. She had heavy black eyebrows—later on, Miss Wilson spent nearly an hour trying to remove those eyebrows—and her full, red lips parted to show a middle tooth or so missing. The girls stared in bewilderment, for they simply couldn't recognise her. Behind her stood a motley throng, all as rigid as possible. A tall slim figure in kilts, with hair powdered and tied back in a queue, and topped by a tam-o'-shanter, was plainly recognisable as Prince Charlie *and* Miss Stewart. Matron, wearing mid-Victorian garb with a cap on her smoothly-banded hair, and bearing a lamp, the English girls knew to be Florence Nightingale. Queen Victoria, too, clad in the flowing white gown portrayed in the picture which shows here at her first council, was quite unmistakable. Little Miss Nalder was, perhaps, rather more tanned than the queen had ever been, but she looked very well for all that.

Then Jo Bettany suddenly cried out, "Oh, Napoleon!" at the figure on the far side, and the girls got a shock as they realised that even the Visiting Staff had been pressed into service, for "Napoleon" was no other than Herr Helfen who came up once a fortnight to give 'cello lessons. But some of the others were not so easily recognised, and a good many of the Continental girls had no idea what it all meant.

It was left to Marie von Eschenau to enlighten them. "Why, it is Mrs. Jarley and the Waxworks we read of in literature two terms ago!" she exclaimed. "But what a clever idea! Only what is going to happen?"

"And who on earth is playing Mrs. Jarley?" demanded Jo perplexedly.

Her clear tones reached the actors, and one or two of them forgot they were waxworks, and grinned involuntarily.

"There is La France," murmured Simone sentimentally. "Ah, la belle France!"

"Don't be soppy!" said Jo austerely. "But doesn't Mademoiselle look jolly!" she added.

At this point, Mrs. Jarley thought it well to open the show, for La France was blushing wildly, and Struwwelpeter was shaking with suppressed laughter. Raising her long wand, she opened her mouth, and gave the original Mrs. Jarley's speech in a deep bass voice, the result of trying to keep down her own giggles.

"*Miss Wilson!*" gasped Frieda. "But I should never have known her!"

"*Bill!*" supplemented Jo. "I say! What a splendid get-up!"

But Mrs. Jarley had finished, and was now bustling round with her wand and a duster, pretending to oil the waxworks, and incidentally seizing the chance to hiss at

80

Aladdin and Struwwelpeter who were rapidly becoming hysterical, "Stop giggling, you two!" in her most ferocious whisper.

Then the show began, and the girls rocked as the show-woman pointed out the awful consequences of not attending properly to one's toilet as evinced by Shock-Headed Peter. Miss Edwards really looked awful; and normally she was the terror of all untidy Juniors! Aladdin was introduced as "a lad of daring and courage, who fears neither man nor beast!" and Cornelia and Co., with vivid recollections of Miss Norman's shrieks when a mouse had been introduced into prep one night, held their sides.

Chopin (the school's eccentric singing-master, Mr. Denny) was, according to Mrs. Jarley, an admirer of sweet, pretty tunes, and Carla and Margia clung together at the description, for if there *was* anything "Plato" hated, it was airs of just that particular type.

Florence Nightingale, so the lady assured the audience, was an excellent nurse, capable of attending to any illness, however bad. and a great believer in the efficacy of *castor-oil*—whereat Joyce, Thekla, and Mary all went scarlet, and Joyce muttered angrily.

They all had a turn, and Miss Wilson showed herself so clever at hitting off weaknesses as well as making sly, topical allusions, that the girls were nearly weeping with laughter before she had got very far. Herr Anserl, the old and hair-trigger-tempered piano-master, who had only the pick of the pupils, received a cheer when he was introduced as the Tyrol's great national hero, Andreas Hofer. Miss Annersley, as Maria-Theresa, Austria's warrior-queen, got another, and remained rigid, for she had an awful feeling that her hair, which had been pinned into ringlets, was gradually escaping its pins, and before long would be lying in its usual straight lengths about her shoulders.

Then a sensation—quite unrehearsed!—occurred. Bonny Prince Charlie, Charlotte Corday, and Garibaldi had been accommodated with seats on a bench that had been set rather near the edge of the platform. Mrs. Jarley bumped against it—she was not accustomed to wearing a train—and it tipped off backwards, bearing with it its occupants who, from the very way they had fallen, were unable to help themselves. So they remembered they were waxworks, and stayed as they were, with only the soles of their feet showing down the side—the bench had been set at the side—whereupon Mrs. Jarley promptly seized the opportunity to read her audience a lecture on how to preserve presence of mind when one's position suddenly became inverted.

Finally, the entertainment wound up with a song which contained solo and chorus, and was the work of the united Staff. It was in English, of course, as the whole show had been, and was accompanied by Chopin, who forgot that he was a dummy, and, as Jo said afterwards, "Spread himself lavishly over the keyboard, just as usual."

Mrs. Jarley opened the ball.

"If some fine or rainy day you find trouble on the way—
Say an unexpected dose of castor-oil—
Or, say, trouble you've been rigging, and you're due to
   get a wigging,
Don't allow yourself to fall into turmoil.
Just pull yourself together, and never mind the weather,
And remember you should never trouble trouble.
Trot out both bright and e-*arly*, and visit Mrs. Jarley,
And she'll provide you with your very double.

Now then, chorus, waxworks!"
The waxworks took it up with a fine vigour.

"So go to Mrs. Jarley on the spot
If your work is wrong or if you've made a blot.
She will straight provide your double
And that little bit of trouble
Disappears; for what *you'd* have, your dummy's got!"

82

Florence Nightingale opened the next verse in her usual crisp manner:

"If in a moment's passion, you should join the ruling
    fashion,
And should bob your hair alone and all unaided,"

Maria-Theresa took it up, while Simone Lecoutier, to whose address this was, went darkly red, and stared straight in front of her:

"Then you suddenly regret, and your family's upset,
And you have no wish your folly be paraded,"

then—

"This needs no peroration. Just call in consultation
Mrs. Jarley; she'll assist you in a trice,"

announced Joan of Arc melodiously; Aladdin following on with—

"And while friends are talking rudely, there's no need to
    go subduedly.
For a dummy ne'er minds chaff, which is so nice!"

"Chorus!" shouted Mrs. Jarley, conducting wildly with her pointer, while Queen Victoria ducked violently to avoid having an eye put out.

"Then go to Mrs. Jarley on the spot
If you've bobbed and later wish that you had not.
Till your hair is grown once more
Keep your dummy to the fore
To take for you the chaff you should have got!"

The last verse was even more strung out in a laudable desire to see that everyone did his or her share toward the gaiety of the evening.

Queen Victoria carolled as a beginning:

"When you've floured your neighbour's hair—"

"When you've tried to prove a chair-
    Back is wider than your friend declares it is—"

chimed in Andreas Hofer with a most unwaxworklike
twinkle.

"If you've giv'n the school a shock by the boiling of
    the clock"

came in muffled tones from the overturned bench where
Garibaldi was nearly suffocated between laughter and dust.

"If you've made bath-water rise up with a fizz,"
declaimed Chopin in his sweetest tenor notes.

"If at Indians you've been playing—"

was La France's contribution.

"If in short you've been a-straying
    From the paths of good and well-conducted youth,"

bellowed Prince Charlie, evidently afraid that he would
never be heard unless he yelled at the top of his voice.
    Maria von Lichtenstein and Rembrandt took up the
tale:

"And you know you're in for trouble, then there's
    nothing like a double
    Made by Mrs. J., and that's the golden truth!"

Finally, the whole party gave the chorus, fortissimo,
and con amore:

"Then go to Mrs. Jarley on the spot,
When you know the water's certain to be hot.
You'll be saved recrimination
By a wax rep-re-sentation
And you'll find that this advice is worth a *lot*;"

Chopin wound up with some striking chords, and the
show was at an end. The girls shouted, though more
people than one looked very sheepish during the song,
and Joey Bettany, as soon as the curtains were drawn together, remarked, "Well, no one can say they've let any
of us off, can they?"

"Simone's hair—" began Frieda.

"To say nothing of the time you and Marie and Jo
floured other folk's hair," added Cyrilla.

"And what price the clock last term?" asked Jo with
a grin.

"It was all good," said Simone with finality in her
tones.—"Oh, what is going to happen now?"

"Refreshments," said Mrs. Jarley, suddenly emerging
from the curtains, her train held well out of the way, and
her bonnet slung by its ribbons over one arm. "Come
along to the Speisesaal, all of you!"

She led the way, escorting La France, to the Speisesaal
where a gorgeous meal was spread. Jellies, creams, fruit,
sweets, chocolates, cakes, and sandwiches of all kinds
covered the table; and there were frothing chocolate with
whipped cream, and iced lemonade to drink. The waxworks waited assiduously on their guests, and saw that
they had a good time.

"Any castor-oil going, Florence?" demanded saucy Jo
of Florence Nightingale as she held out her glass for a
fresh libation of lemonade.

"Plenty in the medicine-cupboard if you'd prefer it to
this," retorted the lady.

"No, thanks; I bar luxuries!" And Jo sipped her
lemonade rapturously.

"Mrs. Jarley, how have you taken out your tooth?" asked Marie.

"Black court-plaster. You surely didn't think I would sacrifice a perfectly good tooth to your amusement?" demanded the lady.

"Oh, *no*! But I wondered how you managed, for, of course, I knew that your teeth were what you had grown," explained Marie, becoming rather confused.

"What *I* should like to know," said Frieda, "is how you are so wide? For if it is cushions, you must be melting."

"It is! And you're quite right, Frieda, I feel suffocated!"

"That's what I felt like, lying upside down like that," sighed Garibaldi—Mr. Denny's sister, who taught Italian and Spanish and advanced German. "I never knew before that dust could be so overpowering."

"Well," said Jo, rising to her feet, her tumbler in her hand, "I think the whole School agrees with me that it's been the best Staff-evening we've ever had. Ladies, I propose the health of Mrs. Jarley and her Waxworks! May *all* their shadows never grow any less! Come along, everyone!"

The girls jumped to their feet, cups and glasses held high. With one voice they shouted out the German toast: "Prosit!"

Then they all drained their cups and glasses, and Marie called on La France to reply.

The lady with the Cap of Liberty perched at a rakish angle on her grey locks rose to her feet. "My dear children, we are so pleased to have pleased you," she said in her own language. "We have enjoyed it as well as you, and we feel that your pleasure has more than repaid us for our work."

"And now," interrupted the Lady with the Lamp, "as it is two hours after the Juniors' bedtime, I'm going to send them off. Some of them are nearly asleep already." She turned to Portia—her colleague who had charge of domestic affairs at Le Petit Chalet—"Matron, will you come?"

Portia nodded. "I quite agree. Come along, little ones; say good-night, and we'll go."

The little ones went obediently. They were all accustomed to rendering the most absolute and cheerful obedience, and on the rare occasions when anyone did rebel, she soon felt herself to be a perfect outcast until she had given in, and all was well again. Florence Nightingale saw them over to their own abode, Struwwelpeter and Aladdin following as soon as they had collected their belongings, and then she came back, and packed off the Middles and the Seniors. It was nearly half-past twenty-two o'clock when the last prefect departed bedwards, and by that time those of the Staff who were not resident had gone too. Finally, Miss Wilson dropped into a chair in the Staff-room, and proceeded to unpack her stuffing while the rest, in various attitudes of weariness, watched her.

"It's been quite a good show," she said as she tossed the last cushion at her great friend, Miss Stewart.—"There you are, Con! And never again, not even for a Staff-evening, will I consent to be padded like this. I should think I must have lost pounds of flesh!"

"You look pounds slimmer," yawned Miss Leslie, getting up from her stool. "Well, I'm for bed. Good-night, everyone! Thank goodness, to-morrow is Sunday, and breakfast is an hour later!"

And as the weary Staff retired to their well-earned rest, they fully agreed with her. Mrs. Jarley had been great fun, but it was a tiring affair.

87

CHAPTER IX

A LITTLE COOKERY

THE Sunday following the Staff-evening went by in peace and quiet. The girls had plenty to discuss in "Mrs. Jarley," and even Thekla the firebrand was quite bland for her. On the Monday, Joyce Linton returned to school, having been kept apart from the others all the previous week until the Saturday. She had had a sharp attack, and, like a good many other highly-strung children, she had complicated matters by running a temperature for the first day or two. Taking into consideration her mother's illness, Dr. Erckhardt thought it better to keep her quiet, and when Dr. Russell—Dr. Jem to the School—came down from the Sonnalpe on the Thursday with a message for his young sister-in-law and heard the whole story, he agreed.

On the Wednesday following, the Lower Fifth took their turn in the Domestic Economy class. This was the fourth since the beginning of term, and they were especially thrilled about it, for they were to start cooking to-day. On the first day they had been instructed in the art of sweeping and dusting. On the second, they had learned how to wash sundry articles, and Frau Mieders, their mistress, had shown them how to starch and iron. This had been a thrilling lesson, for Evadne Lannis used her iron too hot, and the resultant well-toasted camisole had brought shrieks of protest from the mistress. Joyce, on the other hand, had used hers too cold, and *her* garments had looked as if they were rough-dried.

On the previous Wednesday, they had been taught how to clean silver and fine brass, and here Evadne had shone for once, for she owned silver toilet articles and had to keep them clean herself. So she needed little teaching, and the spoons and rose-bowls entrusted to her positively glittered when she had finished with them. They had also learned how to apply blacklead and polishes of that nature, and when Matron saw them afterwards, she ordered them all off to hot baths at once.

But to-day was to come the most exciting thing of all, and the one they had looked forward to with most interest. They were to cook Mittagessen for the entire School. Afterwards, they would be allowed to make cakes for tea; and, of course, they would be shown the most scientific ways of laying tables and washing up. Cooking had been the job of the Sixth Form on the Monday, and the fried fish they had produced had appeared at table in varying stages—from perfectly done fillets to a queer-looking mush which had been Joey's effort.

"Guten Morgen!" said Frau Mieders as they all trooped into the big kitchen. "To-day we cook. Have you then your aprons?"

They had; Matron had seen to that. The girls solemnly arrayed themselves in the big holland overalls, drew on their cooking-sleeves, and tucked their hair away into the close-fitting caps they had brought. Then, after Frau Mieders had inspected their hands, they were told they might begin.

There were fourteen of them, so she set four to peeling potatoes, and four to paring apples, with warnings as to the necessity for taking off only the thinnest paring.

"The best of any fruit lies just beneath the skin," she told them. "Let us see which of you can make the most wafer-like peel."

"What are we to do?" asked Cornelia Flower plaintively.

"Three of you—you, Cornelia, and Ilonka Barkocz and Mercy Barbour, will slice up this cold meat, and again I must ask for wafers," said the mistress. "Come to this table and do it. And Maria, and Frölich, and Olga will peel these onions. Be careful not to hold them too near to your faces or you will weep, for they are very good, strong onions."

"Thank goodness that isn't *our* job!" whispered Evadne to Joyce who was next her. "I *loathe* peeling onions!"

The luckless trio set to work, but before long they were all weeping copiously, and only the awe in which they held the new mistress kept the rest of the form from jeering at them.

"What are we making, Frau Mieders?" asked Lysbet Brandt, a Dutch girl who was more or less possessed of a character, and so dared to draw notice on herself.

"It is a réchauffé," explained Frau Mieders. "Many people think that such must be unpleasant—what you call dull. But if they are carefully prepared and spiced, they may be as savoury as any other dish. And they are also economical."

The girls listened respectfully as they went on with their work, and presently the potato-peelers brought their results to her. She demanded to see the peelings, and Evadne, with great presence of mind, swept the whole lot into one bucket before she could be stopped. She had more than a few qualms as to how Frau Mieders would regard her own work. She was scolded, of course, but the deed was done, and could not be undone. Besides, Frau Mieders did not yet know her Evadne, and it *might* have been the result of enthusiasm. She contented herself by remarking that some of them appeared to be deaf; otherwise, why were some of the peelings of such a thickness?

No one answered her, but two or three people looked at each other guiltily. Frau Mieders nodded, and then turned to the next work. "For our sweet to-day we will make the English apple-pie," she announced.

"Guess it's just as much American as English," murmured Cornelia.

"That's only because the Pilgrim Fathers took the idea

90

over to America with them," said Joyce. "That makes it English all the time."

A withering retort was on the tip of Cornelia's tongue, but Frau Mieders' steel-blue eyes were suddenly fixed on her, and she was obliged to swallow her wrath.

"We must make our pastry presently," she announced when she considered the rebel was sufficiently subdued. "First of all we will quarter the apples and remove the cores, with as little waste as possible, each girl taking four apples. Are they yet peeled? Then do not mix the peelings, but leave them, and I will come and inspect them."

Thanks to this caution, she was able to commend all except Thekla, who considered domestic work of all kinds beneath her, and whose apple-parings would not have compared unfavourably with Evadne's efforts with the potatoes. Thekla went red and looked sulky under the rebuke she received, but rather more than a term at school had at least taught her to receive such things in silence.

"Are the onions finished?" asked Frau Mieders, turning to the three martyrs who were still mopping their streaming eyes.

"This is the last," said Maria Marani.

"Then put them into that saucepan of boiling water, and we will parboil them before we mince them."

The trio thankfully tossed in their onions, and then, by the mistress's orders, retired to rub lemon essence on their hands to remove the smell before they washed them. When they returned, she set them to helping with the apples, and they were all very busy, cutting them into quarters and removing the cores. Some of them did it neatly and efficiently; others who were quite unaccustomed to the work soon had a mangled heap of apple on their chopping-boards. However, it was done at last, and all the apples were put into another saucepan with a little water at the bottom. The lid was put on, and the pan set where it would get only a gentle heat.

"Why do we do that, meine Frau?" asked Maria.

"So that the apples may be pulped. Otherwise we might

have to bake the pies too long for the crust to be light," explained Frau Mieders. "If we considered the crust only then the fruit might not be well cooked. But by stewing them slowly thus, they are pulped before they are put into the dishes, and so we avoid either mistake."

The next thing was to scrub the chopping-boards and set them aside. Then the pastry slabs, all of marble, were produced, and each girl was directed to take a mixing-bowl from the towering pile on the cupboard shelf. When they were ready, Frau Mieders proceeded to give her directions. They weighed out their flour, three girls to each pair of scales. Then they sifted it, adding baking-powder and salt, and then they rubbed in the kneading—half lard and half butter—till it was fine and crumbly.

"Now for the water," said Frau Mieders. "Each of you has a knife for mixing. Add the water little by little till you have a stiff paste that you can roll out readily on your boards. Be careful not to make your paste sticky, or you will spoil it."

They set to work. Some of them followed her instructions with care, and produced pastry of the right consistency. Others added too much, and had to put more flour. Then came the fun of rolling it carefully—"Always *away* from you, else it may become heavy," warned Frau Mieders.

By the time this was all done, the apples were ready. Each girl went in turn and filled her dish with the pulp into which Lysbet had been told to stir brown sugar.— "Brown sugar is best for sweetening purposes," explained Frau Mieders.—Then they went back to their places, ready to fit on their crust.

"But we haven't put any cloves in," protested Joyce at this juncture.

"Cloves? You wish cloves in your English apple-pie?" queried Frau Mieders amiably.

"Oh yes, meine Frau. Or you can use cinnamon," Evadne told her eagerly. "It makes the flavour ever so much nicer!"

"Well, there is no reason why you should not use both. —Cornelia, go to the store cupboard. On the second shelf at the right-hand side you will find the tins. The names are on them—in English, of course."

Cornelia trotted off, and presently returned. By this time, Frau Mieders was at the stove, testing the onions, so she told Cornelia to give two cloves each to half of the girls, and the rest might take half a teaspoonful of the powdered cinnamon to mix with their apple-pulp, so that they should have the two flavours.

"Aren't they big before they're cooked?" said Joyce in surprise as she dropped in her two cloves, and stirred them well among the apples. She lifted her pastry, and laid it over the top, smoothing it down round the greased edges of the pie-dish. "Funny how cooking seems to shrink things, isn't it?"

Cornelia finished her work and took the tins back to the storeroom, that being Frau Mieders' inflexible rule. Otherwise, as she said, the kitchen would soon have been filled up with unnecessary things.

"What a queer, oniony smell there is," commented Maria Marani.

"Frau Mieders has tipped the onions into a strainer," said Lysbet, glancing round. "There! Now I will chop him round in a pattern!" And she proceeded to adorn her pie with neat little strokes.

Frau Mieders left the onions to drain, and came back to the big table to see what her young cooks were doing. "Yes; that is very neat," she said. "Those of you who have not ornamented may do so, and do not forget to make two small holes, one at each side, for the steam to escape."

This was a joyful occupation, and some of those pies were lined and adorned within an inch of their lives. Then they were bidden brush them over with milk so that the pastry would glaze nicely. After that the pies were set on one side till it was time to bake them.

"And now we will proceed with our réchauffé," said

93

Frau Mieders. "Bring the chopping-boards, each take a little of the onions, and mince them finely."

The girls did so, and when the onions were minced, they were put into the pan together with the sliced meat, potatoes (also sliced), herbs chopped to a crumblike fineness, nutmeg, pounded mace, and a sauce compounded of many things. Tomatoes, grown in the garden and preserved the summer before, were added, and then the whole was set in a huge cauldron on the stove to stew slowly.

"Now you may clear everything away," said the mistress, smiling. "We will make our cocoa, and have our Break now."

They turned to with a will, and half an hour later were sipping cocoa that tasted almost like chocolate, and eating crisp little honey-wafers that Frau Mieders had made for them herself. She left them with instructions to see that the stew did not burn, and not to play games, but to talk quietly till she returned. Then she went off to seek her own refreshment.

"I like cooking," said Joyce thoughtfully as she stirred her cocoa. "It will be fun eating the things we've made ourselves. I'm sure those pies will be just as good as the Sixth Form's Apfeltorten!" And she eyed her own particular production proudly.

"What shall we make next?" asked Maria Marani.

"Cakes for Kaffee," said Lysbet.

"I wonder what they will be?" murmured Ilonka Barkocz. "I have helped mamma make our Easter cake, and last Easter she let me try by myself."

"I can make Kappjes," said Lilli van Goeschen, a pretty compatriot of Lysbet's. "Koekjes also."

"Your cakes have such weird names," objected Evadne, who was sitting on the table munching her wafers as if she had had nothing to eat for days.

Lilli laughed. "Not at all. 'Koekjes' are the same as your 'cookies' that I have heard you talk about. Our men who founded New Amsterdam—what you call New York nowadays—took with them their wives, and they made

94

Koekjes for their families. Then when the English came, the word became—became—" she stopped.

"Englished, I suppose you mean," said Evadne calmly. "*I* see! But if you come to that, *I've* made cookies too— at least," she added honestly, "I've had a shot at them."

"How many died?" asked Cornelia.

"Don't worry. Jo and Stacie and I ate the lot. Madame wouldn't let the Robin and the babies have any. They weren't bad, but they *spread* so. They had rather a funny taste, too; but that was because Jo would use the wrong eggs, and some of them were—queer!"

Here the conversation came to an end, for Fräulein entered the room, and the girls had to hurry to clear away their cocoa-mugs, and tidy up generally before they got their mixing-bowls again, and were set to work on their cakes.

Frau Mieders wisely refused to allow them to try anything very elaborate. She insisted on prolonged beating of eggs and butter, though some people complained that their arms ached long before she was satisfied with the results. Finally, fourteen large cakes were put into one of the ovens, while the apple-pies were popped into the other, which had been raked out thoroughly to ensure a good, quick heat so that the pastry would rise.

After that, they had to wash once more, and then go and lay the tables in the Speisesaal. It took some time, for the housemaids were inexperienced, but they contrived to get everything on at last, and then they scampered off to make themselves tidy—but not before time, either. Evadne had to go to Matron with a scorched finger, the result of her own carelessness when opening the oven-door to see how the cakes were getting on, and when Thekla, Joyce, Ilonka, and Maria were dishing up their stew, Thekla contrived to splash some of the boiling gravy over Maria. However, there was no real harm done, and when the School sat down to Mittagessen, the fourteen cooks looked very proudly at the people serving the réchauffé at the heads of the tables.

"I only hope it's safe. I'm not insured, you know," said Jo plaintively as she filled her own plate last, and then tasted gingerly, while Moida, with a suppressed grin, carried off the dish.

"It's as safe as your fish-mess was last week!" cried Evadne indignantly, and Jo subsided as she remembered the horrid mess she had had to dish up.

The réchauffé was voted a complete success, however, and the girls only complained that there hadn't been enough of it.

"Don't be greedy!" said Ilonka severely to Elsie Carr at her table. "There are pies to follow."

"Pies? What kind of pies? Have they provided coal-hammers to chop up the pastry?" demanded Elsie teasingly.

Ilonka's face flamed, but she held her tongue, for at that moment the maids, who had been clearing away the first course, came in, bearing the nicely-browned pies, and proceeded to distribute them.

"How those onions do reek!" said Gillian. "Whatever kind were they, Lonny? I can smell them yet!"

"Frau Mieders said they were very good, strong ones," said Ilonka haughtily.

"They must have been," agreed Marie von Eschenau who headed the table, "only it is not quite an onion smell. It is more—penetrating."

"It's even got into the pies," observed Mary Shaw who was quite recovered now. "Sniff! I don't think I like it!"

There was no doubt about it. The pies—or some of them—*did* smell with a queer, strong scent that was far nearer onions than apples. The mystery was solved when Cornelia who liked delicacies, took a heaped spoonful, choked precipitately, and hid her face in her napkin. Then she jumped up, and without bothering to ask leave of anyone, tore from the room.

"Cornelia!" cried Mademoiselle from her place at the Staff Table. But Cornelia was gone.

"She must have burnt herself," said Miss Wilson,

96

spreading the steaming apple about her plate. "Corney is always in such a hurry. This is flavoured with cinnamon, I can smell, and very nice, too!"

But she got no further, for this was just where a chorus of groans and protests rose.

"Poison! They've been trying to poison us!" proclaimed Jo dramatically.

"Schrecklich!"—"Oh, mais c'est effroyable!"—"Ghastly!" These and other exclamations sounded from all sides. Frau Mieders got up quickly, and went to one of the tables, her face full of distress.

"Jo, let me taste your pie, if you please. Both of ours are flavoured with cinnamon, and, save that the crust is not so light as it might be, are excellent, and I cannot account for this strange odour of—"

She stopped there, and having found a clean spoon, tasted the contents of Jo's plate. The next moment she cast the spoon from her with a shudder. "Garlic! Girls! You have flavoured these pies with garlic!"

"But we could not!" cried Maria protestingly. "There was no garlic—we only used cloves and cinna—"

"Cloves!" The mistress swung round on Cornelia, who had returned just then, looking very much ashamed of herself. "Cornelia, did you take cloves or garlic-cloves?"

Cornelia looked nonplussed. "Guess I just took what there was. It had Cloves on the tin, for I saw it when I got it."

"Go then, and bring me the tin here. Here are the keys."

Cornelia went off meekly, and presently returned with a scarlet face and a large tin which she handed over with the humble statement, "Guess I was in a mite too much of a hurry that time. The cloves were further back on the shelf, and I saw Cloves on this one, and didn't bother to look further."

"Then, girls," said Frau Mieders, her face clearing, "it is all explained. Cornelia has given you garlic-cloves for flavouring instead of plain cloves."

And so it proved. When one of the "cloves" had been rescued from its bed of apple, it turned out to be a clove or pod, of garlic, and this meant that seven pies were so much waste. Luckily, there was enough of those flavoured with cinnamon for everyone to have a small helping, and Mademoiselle had Pflaumetorten brought from the store room to make up for deficiencies.

But never, to the end of her school career, did Cornelia hear the last of her "cloves"!

CHAPTER X

A REGULAR SHOCK

"IF it goes on like this, I can see us having to *swim* up to the Sonnalpe instead of going the usual way. What a downpour! D'you think it's going to be a second Flood?" Joey Bettany turned from the window and looked at the half-dozen people who were with her in the library.

"Oh, I hope not," said Frieda, looking up from the book she had taken from the shelves. "And do tell me, Jo, if *Wintersmoon* is interesting."

"Haven't read it, so don't know. Who wrote it?"

"John Buchan," replied her friend, giving the name a German pronunciation. "I have read of of his before, and liked it. I think I will take this."

"If it's John Buchan's—and I'd advise you to learn to pronounce his name correctly—it's sure to be all right. Will that be enough for the week-end?"

"Oh, quite. I expect I shall spend a great deal of time with Bernhilda, for I have to see their home, and she is not likely to be much with us," said Frieda. "She is keeping very quiet these days."

"I only hope she doesn't mess up your week-end," said her friend. "I remember when David arrived—in the middle of Marie and André's wedding—Dr. Jack came to fetch me because Madge wanted me. It was a pretty trying top-off to the wedding festivities."

"I do not think it at all likely," said Frieda with a smile as she watched Jo enter the name of the book in the register.

"Well, you never know. Hello, Gillian; got yours chosen?"

"Yes. I think I'll try *Le Chat de Madame Michel.* I've never read it, and Mademoiselle Lachenais says my vocab is far too limited even now, and I must read more French. This doesn't look too difficult, so I'll have a shot at it. And may I take *The First Violin* as well? I can't spend the whole Half-term reading French."

"Yes, if you like. Everyone is allowed two books for Half-term if they want them," said Jo. She entered the books, and then went to the window again to look out at the rain streaming down. It had begun on the Tuesday of that week, and had never stopped for more than an hour. The snow was all washed away except in sheltered nooks and hollows, and the ground was being churned to a thick mud of pea-soup consistency. So heavy was the downpour that they were unable to see the lake from the windows, and even the mountains opposite only loomed up as vague shadows.

"It will be difficult getting down to Spärtz," said Frieda pensively.

"Won't it just! The road will be like a morass. Indeed, I shouldn't wonder if you have to take the far side. It's quite likely the stream is out with these floods, to say nothing of the melted snow. Herr Braun was along last night, and he said the stream down yonder was barely a foot below the top of the bank then. I shouldn't be surprised if it flooded before to-night. Thank goodness we moved the library up here at the beginning of term!"

"Well, if it does flood, we shall all be away by evening," said Marie von Eschenau comfortably. "Only another two hours before we go!—I will take these, Joey, though I do not expect to do much reading, for Wanda wrote in her last letter that there is a good opera company at Salzburg, and Friedel will engage seats for us for to-morrow night and also on Monday."

Jo returned to her register, and scribbled the names of the books Marie held out to her. Evadne Lannis turned from the shelves at the same moment, and brought hers, though she, like Marie, expected to attend the opera, for

100

her people were now living in Salzburg, not far from where the von Glucks had their home. The other two people, Thekla von Stift and Joyce Linton, chose their volumes, and when Thekla's had been entered, she departed. The rest stayed to talk. Mademoiselle had said that as the weather was so bad, there would be no lessons that morning, but they would start from the school at noon instead, and she advised the girls to take library-books with them in case the rain continued. Everyone was going away this Half-term, and the school would be deserted. She and the Staff and most of the Seniors were busily clearing all books and furniture out of the ground-floor rooms in case of accidents. During its first year, the Chalet School had been badly flooded, and though the bed of the stream which ran into the lake from the mountains had been deepened, and the banks artificially raised, while a deep ditch had been dug all round the Chalet School estate to carry off any water, still, the torrents of rain they had been having made it not at all unlikely that there would be a second edition of that experience. The valley folk were becoming uneasy, and some of those who lived near the banks of the stream had already taken their valuables to the houses of friends who lived further off.

"What a lark it would be if we got down on Tuesday and found the whole place flooded out!" said Joyce, who was perched on the arm of her sister's chair.

"Don't suppose for a moment they'd allow us to come down if that happened," said Jo amiably. "In that case, my child, we'd get a day or two extra, for they'd never bring us into a damp house."

"But how could we know?" demanded Gillian.

"Oh, they'd 'phone us, of course," said Jo. "No one is going frightfully far away. Even Thekla is only going to Innsbruck to visit her old aunt. And of course, the people from other countries are all off to Kufstein if they aren't going home with friends, and Herr Braun would let them know. He'd ring us up at the Sonnalpe, too."

101

"A lot of use that would be if the wires are still down," Gillian reminded her. "Mademoiselle was at it again when I came up to change my book, and nothing had been done then. I rather think she wants to get through to your sister."

"I know—to ask her advice in case of flooding," said Jo cheerfully. "It *is* a nuisance the wires going just this minute. I wanted to let them know they could expect me earlier than usual, but we couldn't do a thing. I don't suppose they'll bother about it either, while this weather lasts. It's only a private line, you know. The public one goes the other way."

"Can't they put you through on that?"

"Only from Spärtz. Oh, well, it doesn't really matter."

"How many of us *are* going to the Sonnalpe?" asked Gillian.

Jo considered. "Let me see. You two and myself—three. Elsie Carr and Maria Marani—five. Ruth Wynyard, Vi Allison, Corney, and Biddy O'Ryan—nine. That's all, I think. I wish you'd been coming, Frieda."

"Oh, I must see Bernhilda," laughed Frieda. "And Gisela has Maria and Gillian and Joyce staying with her, so I am sure she will not miss me for once."

"Only Biddy and me going to 'Die Rosen,'" said Jo. "My sister wouldn't let me ask anyone else, though I rather wanted Corney. But she said she'd rather not when I was up and asked her. She said she wanted to be quiet for once. Can't think what's happening to her—it's not like her to be stodgy."

"Where's Corney going, then?" demanded Joyce.

"The Carrs asked her to go to them. The other babes will be with their people at the hotel. Oh, well, there'll be plenty to do. All the nursery folk will keep me busy; and I expect we'll have a tamasha of some kind at 'Die Rosen' before the hol's over."

"I hope it's not raining like this up there," said Gillian with an involuntary shiver. "It'll be so cold and miserable for invalids."

"Don't worry about that. They may be right above the clouds—they often are. Remember they are nearly four thousand feet higher than we are, and often have the most glorious sunshine when we're going round with macs and brollies," said Jo comfortingly. "Well, I wonder if you folk are the last for library.—Joyce, you might go and see if anyone else is coming, will you? If not, I want to shut up."

Joyce went off, and presently returned to say that everyone who wanted books had got them, and Mademoiselle said Jo was to go and help move the things from the "chemmy lab," and Gillian, Frieda, and Marie were to go with her.

Jo nodded her thanks; put the odd books away; closed and locked the doors of the cupboards, and then, having seen them out of the room, shut that door too, and went off downstairs, whistling like a blackbird.

From then until noon, when the last of the girls and staff to leave the school assembled at the gate, life was too full for much chattering. By that time, however, the downstairs rooms had all been stripped, and everything was in order as far as possible. The fires in the stoves had all been raked out, and all doors locked. Mademoiselle Lepâttre, who was to spend the holiday at the Annexe, fastened the gate, and then marshalled her party into line, and led them along the lake-path. At Seespitz, the tiny hamlet at the foot of the lake, they were to be met by a motor-bus; but just here the path was too narrow, even for a small car, so the girls, well wrapped up, with wellingtons, oilskins, and sou'-westers, had to tramp through the liquid mud, which they did with many a groan.

"I do think it might have cleared up till we got away," said Jo. "This weather is disgraceful! I've never known it like this before—not in all the years I've lived here!"

"How long is that?" asked Gillian, who was with her.

"Five or thereabouts. I was twelve when we came—not thirteen till the November—and I'm seventeen now. What fun it was! I've always been happy here; but sometimes I

103

think that first term was the best of all!" And Jo wagged her head with a grandmotherly air. "We were all new together, you see, and Bernie—that's Frieda's sister, you know—and Grizel (who is music-mistress at the Annexe now), and Juliet (who is Head there), and Gisela (whom you're going to stay with) were all with us. Gisela was head-girl, and in some ways the best we've ever had. Simone and Frieda and I were Middles, and Maria was a Junior—the only one we had at first. Remind me some time, Gill, and I'll tell you about it."

"I will," said Gillian. "But it's a top—I mean a jolly nice school now, Joey. If it weren't for Mummy, I'd be awfully glad to be here."

"But your mother is getting on," urged Joey. "You said yourself the last time you were up that she seemed stronger."

"Yes; I know. But oh, Joey, you don't know what it's like to know she's so terribly ill!"

"Perhaps not. But I know what I felt last summer when they thought the Robin was going to be bad." Jo's face clouded at the remembrance. "And I remember what a blue funk I was in when David was born. Madge was pretty ill then, you know."

"I suppose she—Mrs. Russell, I mean—is almost like your mother," said Gillian thoughtfully.

"The only mother I've ever known. Mine died when I was born, and father before that," said Jo. "Madge and Dick—that's her twin brother, and Rix and Peggy's father—brought me up between them."

"Then she must have been just like a mother," decided Gillian. "Still, she's all right now; and Mummy was ever so much better when I was last up."

"Hello! So you've got here safely after all? We wondered if you'd all be washed away," said a cheery voice at this juncture, and the two girls jumped, for they had not seen Dr. Russell bearing down on them.

"Jem!" cried his sister-in-law, "how on earth did you know we were coming early?"

"Mademoiselle rang up Herr Anserl, and he rang *us* up," replied the doctor.

"Oh! I see. Isn't this *awful* weather? Don't tell us you've got it too."

Jem Russell shook his head. "You've got a hope, haven't you? It's been pouring on and off for the last three days. The garden is a bog, and no one has been able to put a nose out of doors except Humphries and my noble self. We even had to take the car to bring the Robin to 'Die Rosen' this morning—daren't let her risk the ten minutes' walk in this." Then he turned to slim, blue-eyed Gillian, who was looking at him very wistfully. "Well, Gillian, I expect you want to hear how your mother is. She's very well, all things considered. Of course, we've had to keep her indoors the last few days, but she's sleeping well, and eating well, and she's gained steadily since last you were up."

"Oh, Dr. Jem!" Gillian's face was flushed like a rose, and stars shone in her eyes.

He laughed, and then turned aside to greet Mademoiselle and the others. Jo stared after him, a puzzled look on her face. "There's something up," she said aloud.

Gillian roused from her rapture of joy to look at her. "How do you mean?" she asked. "What could possibly have happened?"

"Jem looks as if he'd come into an unexpected fortune," returned Jo. "I wonder what's happened?"

"I heard nothing when I was up a fortnight ago," began Gillian.

But Jo was not listening. She had darted back to drag her brother-in-law to one side and ask imperiously, "Jem! What's happened?"

He glanced round. The rest were climbing into the big bus, and they were quite unnoticed at the moment.

"You've got a new niece, Joey," he said quietly.

"*What?*" gasped Jo incredulously. "Do you mean— Madge?"

"Well, who else should I mean, you goat?"

105

"But nobody said anything when I was up at the Annexe last month."

"Well, the lady wasn't expected yet, and Madge didn't want you told too soon beforehand. She did try to hint at it, but you didn't take it in. Anyhow, the infant arrived quite unexpectedly last night—kept me out of bed the whole blessed night into the bargain. Madge is all right, and the baby is a jolly mite—though I think you'll get quite a surprise when you see her." He paused to grin, and Jo opened her lips to ask a question, but he went on quickly, "You'll all have to think up some sort of name for her. The second is to be Margaret, of course; but we've got a Madge and a Peggy already, so we thought we'd like to have a change. I propose we have a name-party before the week-end is over, and then you can all say what you would like."

"But I can't think how——" began Jo.

"My dear, do try to realise that we haven't really seen you since Christmas. It's a month since you were up, and then you were at the Annexe, and only came over on the Sunday afternoon. Besides, as I've told you before, she wasn't expected till the end of April. You're late with Half-term, by the way, aren't you?"

"Yes; I know. It's partly with Easter being so late, and partly because we are only going to have a week then, and finish summer term at the end of June. Mademoiselle thinks it will be better if we have long holidays in the hot weather. You know what it was like last summer."

"I agree with her. Well, suppose you get into the bus, now? The rest are all in, and we seem to be keeping them waiting. By the way, we've told no one yet—not even the Robin; so keep it to yourself for the present."

Jo nodded, and climbed meekly into the bus, and took her seat. He followed her, and then the door was shut, and the driver set off along the wide road that had been levelled at this part till the road joined the broad coach-road that ran from Wiesing. All this time, Joey remained in a brown study, and not even Cornelia could get her to talk. Finally, they left her to herself, and chattered among themselves like so many magpies. Gillian alone wondered what had happened to silence the head-girl, for Jo was a talkative young woman as a rule.

"When can we see Mummy, Dr. Jem?" demanded Joyce as the great motor swung into the Wiesing road, and turned upwards to the alm.

"This afternoon, I hope," he said. "She rests till half-past three, and then, if she is all right, you are to go and have tea with her. Frau Mensch will look after you till then."

"What?" exclaimed Joey, roused from her brooding by this. "Is Tante Gretchen up *here*?"

"Tante Gretchen up here?" repeated the doctor. "Of course she isn't! She's in Innsbruck. What on earth makes you ask such a stupid question?"

"Well, you said— Oh! I see! I always forget that Gisela is Frau Mensch, too. Oh, dear! How fearfully elderly it does make her seem!"

The doctor chuckled. "Not got over your aversion to growing up *yet*? It's time, isn't it? You're getting on for eighteen, and will leave school at the end of next term."

"I'm not eighteen till November, and this is only March," said Jo shortly. "Besides, I didn't mean that, exactly, either. Only, Gisela seems so *young* to be called just the same as Tante Gretchen."

"Mamma was no older when she was born," remarked Maria Marani, sister of the aforementioned Gisela. "After all, Joey, Gisela is twenty-two next month, and Baby Natalie is a year old then, too."

"And Davie is two in May, and now—" Jo suddenly stopped short. If there had not been a little excitement just then, she would certainly have been teased to finish her sentence; but just at that moment the bus skidded half-way across the road, and in the resultant panic her remark was forgotten. When they got straight again, and were once more climbing steadily up the hill, the girls were eagerly discussing how they would spend their holiday, and Jo, thinking she had better try to forget what was waiting for her at home, joined in.

They were nearly at the top of the road now, and it was still raining, though the girls from the valley declared that it was not coming down nearly so heavily as in the Tierntal.

"I believe it *is* looking a little better," conceded the doctor, "so perhaps it may stop presently. But you won't be able to get out very much—unless we get blazing sunshine and a good high wind to dry up the mud."

"Well, we might," said Jo optimistically. "You never can tell."

"Is Bette coming to see us?" demanded Cornelia of the doctor.

"I don't doubt she would if she could," he said. "Unfortunately, Bette was hanging up fresh curtains two days ago, and the steps slipped, and she fell, so that she is laid up with a sprained ankle."

"Who is she?" asked Joyce in a whisper of Violet Allison who was sitting next her.

"Signora di Bersetti," returned Violet. "She was at school—oh, before I came. She was Bette Rincini then. She's cousin to Anita and Giovanna, and was one of the first girls, like Gisela Mensch and Frieda's sister Bernhilda. She married Dr. Bersetti last summer, and he is one of the doctors at the Sanatorium."

"What is she like?"

"Oh, ever so nice! Didn't you see her when you were here before term began?"

Joyce shook her head. "No; Joey said we should, but if it's Signora di What's-her-name, she got a wire the day we arrived to say that her father was very ill and she must go at once, and she didn't come back all the time we were at 'Die Rosen.' "

"I see. Well, she's ever so nice, and so pretty, too," said Violet. "She talks English as well as we do. You'll like her, Joyce."

"Oh, I don't suppose I'll see much of anyone," said
108

Joyce. "Gill and I will be at the San most of the time."

"Will you?" said Dr. Russell, overhearing this. "I'm afraid not, Joyce. Your mother is much better, but she can't bear very much yet. You and Gillian shall visit her every afternoon for a short while, but that's all we can permit, I'm afraid."

Joyce's lips drooped, and the tears came to her eyes. "Oh! And I was so looking forward to telling her everything!"

"I must have a chat with you two," he said gently. "However, there will be plenty of time for that. Here we are at the top, and it won't be very long before we are at home.—We'll go straight to 'Das Pferd,' I think, Maria, and hand you three over to Gisela.—Elsie, we can drop as we pass—and you hotel people, as well. Then Jo and I will go back to 'Die Rosen.'"

"Oh, drop me at the gate," implored Jo.

He shook his head. "No fear! I'm not going to have you rushing in and raising the place, as you will do if I'm not there to restrain you. It won't make ten minutes' difference, because Gisela will be on the outlook for her visitors, and Elsie and Co. we'll just dump."

"Thank you!" retorted Elsie, who was an old friend of his. "All the same," she added, "it's jolly nice to think we're in our own house. I'm ever so glad Dad and Mother decided to build up here. It makes such a topping holiday for Dad when he gets leave—much better than England at present."

"Well, it's giving Lilias more time here," agreed the doctor. "She really is a credit to us, Elsie."

By this time they were running along a narrow path which led round a small spur of the mountain. Then the roadway widened, till they reached a broad shelf at the entrance to which stood the two churches, one Catholic, the other Anglican, with the tiny presbyteries belonging to each facing each other. Mr. Eastly and Vater Ambrosius were great friends, and it was necessary to have some form of Protestant worship up there, as many of the patients and their friends belonged to one branch or another of the Protestants. A kind of straggling street followed, lined on either side with chalets and one or two small shops. Each chalet had its own garden, which, in the season, was a blaze of colour, though at present they had nothing to show. At the end of the street was the big hotel, the "Goldener Apfel," where the friends and relatives of patients lived.

Further up the road, on the opposite side, stood the large bungalow Elsie's parents had built, and here Elsie and Cornelia were dropped. The girls for the hotel had already been met by Mrs. Allison, a slim, anxious-faced woman, whose husband was an inmate of the Sanatorium. Further on, Joey pointed out to Gillian and Joyce the pretty chalet where the Di Bersettis had their home. Then they came to a place where the road divided, and turned off to the right, and round a spur of the mountain, and so reached "Das Pferd," the home of Dr. Mensch and his pretty wife and their precious small daughter.

Here Maria and the Lintons were decanted, and their luggage handed over to the sturdy Tyrolean girl who came to get it. Then the bus was carefully backed and turned, and in five minutes Joey was leaping out of it and flying up the path at "Die Rosen," regardless of the streaming rain, her umbrella left behind her, and her case dropped on the ground into all the mud.

She was met at the door by a big, jolly-faced woman in nurse's uniform.

"Well, Jo," said this person, "how are you?"

"Oh, let me go to Madge!" pleaded Jo.

Nurse refused to budge an inch, however. "Mrs. Russell is asleep, and I'm not going to have you waking her up. Besides, look at the mess you are in! And all wet with rain, too! No, my dear; you can go quietly to your bedroom and change into something dry—shoes and stockings, too, mind—and then go to the nursery till I call you."

Jo pulled a face. "Can't I just peep at her through the door? I'll be as quiet as a mouse—honour bright, I will."

"No; certainly not. Now do as I tell you, Jo, and don't argue. Besides, if your sister sees you like that, she'll begin to worry in case you catch cold, and that will be very bad for her," she added, thus clinching the matter.

Jo scowled, but she went off to her room, where she changed rapidly into the things she always kept at the Sonnalpe, and then she went along to the nursery, where she was greeted with cries of rapture from her little adopted sister, Robin Humphries, and her small nephew and niece, Peggy and Rix Bettany, and also from Madge's small son, David. A quieter welcome came from Stacie Benson, who was now sitting upright in her invalid chair. Stacie at once proceeded to announce that she was able to walk a few steps already and hoped soon to be done with the chair altogether.

"No!" Jo was suitably impressed. "I say, how perfectly splendid! And when can you come back to school?"

Eustacia turned questioning eyes on the doctor, who had followed his sister-in-law into the room in time to hear her question.

"This is March," he said thoughtfully. "When does the summer term start, Jo?"

"On the fifth of May," said Jo promptly.

"The fifth of May? H'm! That makes—let's see—just about eight weeks ahead. Well, if you continue to go on as well as you're doing, Stacie, I see no reason why you should not go down for the summer term—how long will *that* be, Jo?"

"Begins on the fifth of May; ends on the ninth of July," said Jo. "Just about nine weeks, isn't it?"

"About that, I think. Well, Stacie, I don't think there ought to be any reason why you can't go down and see what you can do, at any rate. You'll have to go slowly at first, and, of course, there must be no running about. But you get into working order, and then the long summer holiday will probably leave you almost as fit as ever."

"Oh, *good*!" said Jo enthusiastically. "And now, Jem, *can't* I go and see Madge?"

111

"Auntie is ill," said Peggy, slipping a hand into her young aunt's. "Nursie is wif her."

"She's better now," said Jem Russell. "Yes, Joey; she was rousing up when I looked in a moment ago, so if you will be very good and quiet, you may go in for five minutes."

"Me too," pleaded the Robin, lifting her lovely little face coaxingly to his. "I do want to see Tantie Guito."

"Not this time, mein Vögelein. Tante Guito must be quiet and not have too much chattering. So we will let Joey have first turn, and you shall go next."

"An' ven us?" pleaded Peggy.

"Yes; one at a time, though.—Run along, Joey, and when you come back, you can tell the others all the news," he added with a twinkle in his eye.

Jo needed no second bidding. She raced off, and was presently tapping at a door at the far end of the corridor of the opposite wing of the house. Nurse opened it, and nodded with a smile. "Yes; come in—but only for five minutes; and I'll show you the baby."

"Indeed, I'll show her Baby myself," said a dear voice from the bed near the window. "As if anyone but myself should show Joey my daughter!"

Jo went quietly across the room, and dropped on her knees by the side of the low bed, her black eyes, deep love glowing in them, searching the pale face on the pillows. "Madge, darling! This is the shock of my life!"

"Well, I did try to hint the last time I saw you," said her sister, "but you were most unaccountably *thick*, Joey! And besides, we didn't expect her Babyship for another seven weeks or so. It was quite a shock to *me* when she arrived. Kiss me, darling, and then Nurse shall bring Babs here and I'll show her to you."

The sisters kissed tenderly, and then Nurse came across the room with a bundle carefully rolled in flannel in her arms, and laid it down beside Mrs. Russell. "There you are," she said. "There's your precious daughter!"

Eagerly Jo bent over the bundle and scanned the tiny,

112

puckered-up face. The next moment, all caution forgotten, she had jumped to her feet.

"Madge Russell!" she cried in tones of deepest outrage. "That kid of yours has *red hair*!"

"Yes; won't she make a lovely contrast with Davie?" said the baby's mother contentedly. "He is so dark, and she is obviously going to be so fair."

"But carrots!" protested Jo.

Madge Russell flung her sister a look of indignation. "It *isn't* carrots—it's a beautiful Titian red! You don't deserve to have a niece!"

"That's quite enough excitement," said Nurse, taking command. "Off you go, Jo. There's the gong for Mittagessen, anyway. You can break the news to the rest, and be thinking up a name for your new niece."

Stunned, Jo left the room, to go and announce to the expectant party she had left, "I've got a new niece—Davie has a sister! And her hair is plain *ginger*!"

CHAPTER XI

THE BABY'S NAME-PARTY

DURING that Friday night the wind rose and drove the clouds away with a mighty gale that blew so strongly all Saturday that no one was able to go out. The Lintons had been able to take tea with their mother the previous afternoon, but on Saturday they were obliged to ring up the Sanatorium to say that they couldn't get there. Dr. Gottfried, as they were told to call Dr. Mensch, assured them that it was all he could do to keep his feet, and they would have been blown over before they had gone a dozen yards away from the door. Up there on the alm they caught the full force of it, and he was going to spend the day at the Sanatorium to avoid going and coming.

Towards evening the gale fell, and when Sunday came it came with bright sunshine and sabbath peace. The girls all went to church, and Jo enjoyed herself enormously by expatiating on the redness of her new niece's hair. In the afternoon, the Lintons were able to spend the whole time with their mother, who was more and more charmed with the effect the Chalet School seemed to be having on them both. Gillian was beginning to find herself, and not be content to remain so much in the background. Joyce appeared to have a little thought for other people. Both had lost a good deal of their slang—she had no idea that it was the result of finding themselves penniless week after week that had done it—and both seemed very happy where they were.

On the Monday, they were all invited to "Die Rosen" to Kaffee und Kuchen, where they made the acquaintance of Miss Russell, and admired the beautiful mop of thick, coppery curls that adorned her little head, and cried out with delight at the deep blue of her eyes.

"They may change, though," said Joey, who was holding her. "David's eyes were blue when he first came, but they soon turned brown. So Baby's may, though I hope they won't. Jem has blue eyes, so let's hope she inherits them from him."

"What a contrast she makes with David!" said Stacie Benson from her chair. "Bring her here, Jo, and let me hold her."

Joey gave her the baby with a warning to be careful, and Joyce slipped down on her knees before the chair to examine the tiny feet beneath the white draperies.

"Oh, *aren't* they darling!" she said adoringly.

"Yes; aren't they?" said Jo. "Give her to me now, Stacie. We mustn't keep her here any longer. Nurse said only ten minutes."

She took the baby, carefully wrapping the soft shawl round her, and drawing the little house-cap closer round the tiny face. Gillian helped her to adjust the veil which shielded the baby's eyes from the light, and then the young aunt bore off her precious burden to the big bedroom where Madge Russell was awaiting the return of her daughter.

"We're to find a first name for her," said the young aunt when she got back to the nursery where they were all assembled. "The second is to be Margaret after her mother, of course. But we don't want to use it; so all put your brains in steep, and see what you can hunt up. It must be something pretty."

"But why not Josephine for you?" suggested Maria.

Jo shook her head. "No fear! One in the family is quite enough, thank you! Besides, what could you call her?' Josephine is miles too long for such a babe, and I hate Josie. No; try again, Maria."

"What about your mother's name?" suggested Gillian.

"Same as my sister's. And so was Jem's mother. They were both Margaret. And his only sister is Margot, and though we've never seen her—she lives in Australia—we can't use that. And *her* little girl is Daisy. So that about settles any abbreviations for Margaret."

"Guess you'd better call her after the saint of the lake," suggested Cornelia cheerfully.

"No *fear*!" cried Jo. "Scholastika, indeed! Poor lamb! It's as well *you* haven't the final choice if *that's* your idea of names!"

"Why not Evangeline?" asked Elsie Carr.

"Make it Vaseline and have done with it!" retorted Jo. "Besides, it always makes me think of that sickening Little Eva in *Uncle Tom's Cabin*. No; we'll bar luxuries, I think."

"I know—call her after Elisaveta, and ask Veta to be her godmother. Then if ever Veta is queen of Belsornia, she'll have a queen for her godmother, and that would be so nice." This was Violet Allison's bright idea.

But once more Jo put a damper on it. "My dear Vi! Have you forgotten that Veta is a Catholic and we aren't? Catholics can't godma Protestants."

"I didn't know that," said Violet, who was a great admirer of the little Crown Princess of Belsornia, who, two years or so before this, had spent two happy terms as a schoolgirl at the Chalet School, and who had shared in the Guide Camp which had taken place in the summer.

"Well, it is so. So that idea's no good. Think again!"

"What are you being so scathing about?" demanded Dr. Russell, coming in on them at this moment.

"We're trying to choose a name for Babs," explained Jo. "Unfortunately, no one seems able to do anything but make the maddest suggestions."

"Well, what's your own idea?" he asked as he sat down and lifted his small son to his knee.

"We-ell, I rather think I should like Malvina. It's not common, and Malvina Russell makes quite a pretty combination."

"And what price Malvina Margaret Russell?" demanded the doctor, pulling one of his son's curls.

116

"Well, it's not too bad."

"It's as bad as Evangeline would ever have been," put in Elsie as a slight recompense for Jo's snub.

"Good Heavens! You weren't proposing to give my daughter such a name as that?" he asked. "Here, Davie, what shall we call sister?"

"Wufie," said David, wriggling to get down.

"Ruth? That's not a bad idea."

"Not Wufe—Wufus," returned the cherub, now on the floor once made and sidling over to his cousin Rix, who regarded him with a lofty air of contempt.

"Oh, my aunt! He means Rufus!" gasped Jo.

"We'll see what the rest of the babies have to say," chuckled her brother-in-law. "Here Peggy, what would you like to call your new cousin?"

"Florentina," said Peggy rapturously. "Jus' like my new lollie!"

The girls went into fits of laughter, and the doctor called up the manly Rix and asked what name he would like to bestow on his small cousin.

"She's only a girl," quoth Master Rix, who was passing through a period of great scorn for most of the gentler sex. "I don't care!"

"Rude little brute!" commented his aunt.

"Nonsense, Jo! It's just the result of being with so many girls. David is too young to be much of a companion to him yet. Now, Rix," went on Jem, turning to his nephew, "I want you to choose a name, so be quick and do it."

Rix knew that his uncle always meant what he said, so he cocked his head on one side and thought. Finally, "Call it Tibby," he announced.

In the middle of the shrieks of laughter this brought, Rosa, the nurse, appeared with the little ones' Kaffee—in their case, hot milk—and the gong sounded to bring the elders down to the salon for theirs.

When they were all settled, Dr. Jem began again. "I

117

told Joey we'd have a name-party. This is it, so each of you can choose a name, and we'll discuss them all."

"The youngest begin," said Jo, waving her jug of milk wildly in the air. "What do *you* choose, Robinette?"

The Robin considered. "Me, I like Marya because it was Mamma's name," she said at last.

But the doctor refused to consider it. "No, Robin. We aren't going to have two M's before the surname. So think again, pet."

The Robin thought hard, a piece of cake half-way to her mouth, while the rest sipped their coffee and enjoyed the little cakes which had come from Innsbruck that morning.

"I think Angel would be very pretty," said the small girl at last.

"Too much strain on the poor babe!" said Joey decisively. "Fancy having to live up to a name of that kind!"

A good deal of this was Greek to the Robin, so she sat placidly, nibbling at her cake, and the doctor turned to the next youngest member of the party, Biddy O'Ryan.

Biddy was a wild, Irish scamp. The daughter of a sergeant who had died when she was small, she had been brought to the Tyrol by her mother, who had gone back to her former mistress as lady's-maid, and when the lady had died, the maid had married the Italian chauffeur. Both of them had died, leaving ten-year-old Bridget, an orphan in a strange land, with only the prospect of the Cecilia Home before her. She had run away from Hall where she had been living, and had wandered up to the Tiernsee, where seven naughty Middles of the Chalet School—among them Elsie Carr and Cornelia Flower—had adopted her. Luckily for all concerned, the plan was discovered, and Biddy was legally adopted by the Guides. She was sent first of all to the village school at St. Scholastika's at the head of the lake; but she soon proved that she would require more education than she would get there. So, after much consultation, it was agreed that she should come to the school, and already she was showing progress. She could speak French and German fluently now; and her English, once rich with a Kerry brogue, was becoming more standardised, thanks to examples, lectures, and fines.

"Sure, after Mary, there isn't a name to beat Honor—like Miss Honora me mother was maid to," she said now.

"It's such a stiff sort of name," protested Joey. "Still, you could always shorten it to Honor, I suppose."

"That was the way with Miss Honora," agreed Biddy cheerfully.

"Then stick it down as Honor, Jem," ordered his sister-in-law.

Dr. Russell meekly did as he was told, and then looked at Ruth, the next in age. Now Ruth Wynyard was, to outward view, merely a jolly tomboy, and as matter-of-fact a child as you could find anywhere. So it came as a distinct shock to those who thought they knew her when she said wistfully, "Do you know, I've always wanted to know someone called Esmeralda. I think it's such a lovely name!"

"Esmeralda Margaret—help!" said Joey when she had got her breath again. "You don't want to burden the poor mite at all, do you?"

"Well, Dr. Jem asked for our favourite names," argued Ruth. "That's mine, and I don't see that it's any worse than that awful Malvina of yours."

"Dry up!" ordered the doctor. "If you two want to scrap, you can go elsewhere to do it. All right, Ruth, I've put it down.—Violet, you're next—and don't suggest either Victoria or Alexandra, as you seem keen on queens' names!"

Shy Violet coloured, but she stood to her guns. "It was only because of Veta," she said sturdily. "But if you want to know, my *favouritest* name is Rosalind, 'cos of Rosalind in *As You Like It*. I think it's a lovely name."

119

"Well, it's passable, anyhow," said Jo the exigent. "Who's next?"

"Maria," said the doctor. "Come along, Maria; out with it!"

"I like Otillie best," said Maria calmly.

Jo pretended to swoon. "The trouble with you people is that you're coming over all romantic," she declared as she sat up in response to a jerk from Jem. "Joyce, it's you next, and do, for goodness' sake, see if you can tone things down a little."

"It's no use giving my favourite name," said Joyce dejectedly, "because Dr. Jem said he didn't want any more M-names. My second favourite is Anstice."

"What's the first?" asked Cornelia curiously.

"It's Marigold. I do think it's the prettiest name there is."

"Well, I guess it's just as well Dr. Jem put a stopper on *that*! Marigold Margaret! Gee, what an awful mix-up!"

"Well, is yours any better?" demanded Joyce.

"It's not my turn yet. Gillian comes before me. You'll hear it all in good time. Anyway, it isn't a sickly sentimental name; I'll tell you that much! Malvina—Otillie—Esmeralda! Huh!" Cornelia finished up with an indescribable sound.

"I only thought of Malvina because I've been reading about one, and I thought it would be rather uncommon," protested Jo.

"Well, I've been reading about a Volumnia—I've been reviving my memories of Shakespeare—but I've no intention of calling my daughter that," said the doctor. "In any case, it sounds more like a steamer than a small girl. And Malvina is nearly as bad. However! Come along, Gillian. Let's hear the worst."

"I rather like the old-fashioned names like Faith and Prudence," replied Gillian. "I know Jo will have a fit at that, but I do."

"If you call the babe Faith, she'll turn out the most unbelieving creature in creation," protest Jo. "And Mercy is

120

enough to make her the most pitiless wretch under the sun! Do give us a change, Gill!"

"Well, then, what about Loveday? *That's* pretty, and uncommon, too."

"All right," said the doctor. "I'll put that down.—Now, Corney—and let me warn you in advance, young woman, that the baby won't be christened either Nokomis or Minehaha to please you, so keep off Indian names."

"Shouldn't give them, either," returned Cornelia. "I like plain names best, and so would you if you had a name like mine. Jane is my pick."

Down it went, though Jo pulled a face, and murmured, "Jane Margaret! Well, that's about the limit!" Then the doctor turned to Stacie, who was sitting listening with many chuckles. "Now, Stacie?"

"I like either Anne or Katharine, and either would go with Margaret, and they are plain, but not too plain," she said.

"Quite right. It's Elsie's turn now.—Give me some coffee, Jo, while she is making up her mind.—Well, Elsie?"

"You know," said Elsie conversationally, "I always like girls' names that come from boys. Robin, for instance; she has a charming name. And then Joey's Josephine is so pretty, and it's from Joseph."

"Well, you can't call the poor babe Jemima just because of that," protested Joey.

"Haven't you any other name, Dr. Jem?" asked his guest.

"Yes; but if you think I'll agree to Wilhelmina any more easily than to Jemima, you'd better guess again," he retorted.

"Oh, well, it was only a suggestion. However, I think I'll say Dorothea. It has a nice meaning, and it's not so ordinary as Dorothy. The worst of it is, they'll all call it Dorotea here, which spoils it."

"Righto; I've got it down.—Now, Joey! You've been critical enough with other people, so we shall expect something outstandingly good from you," declared the doctor. "What's your choice?"

"I vote for Clare.—Not Clara, mind.—I hate that, and always did. We once had a maid called Clara in England when I was tiny, and she was a bad-tempered cat," said Jo viciously. "But I do like Clare, and it doesn't go too badly with Margaret, either."

The doctor scribbled it down, and looked at his list. "Well, I must say you've shown some ingenuity among the lot of you. Just listen to your selections!" And he read them out: "Angel—Honor—Esmeralda—Rosalind — Otillie — Anstice — Loveday — Jane — Anne or Katharine—Dorothea—and Clare."

"Which will you choose?" asked Gillian eagerly.

"Can't tell you yet. I must see what my wife says. After all, we've plenty of choice here, and I dare say we shall get something out of it. Personally," he went on gravely, "I'm in favour of christening her Esmeralda Margaret Honor Angel. It would be unique, anyhow—Joey, put that cushion down! Do you want to smash anything?"

"It's a good thing for you that we're having Kaffee und Kuchen," retorted Jo as she laid down the cushion she had poised threateningly. "As for the name, it's my belief you've been pulling our legs all this time."

"I shouldn't dream of doing such a thing. My dear Jo, what a suggestion?" And he got up, and quitted the room somewhat hastily, leaving the girls looking at each other. He came back to say, "If you've all finished, I think it would be as well to ring for Marie to clear."

Jo stretched out her hand and rang the bell for Marie, once at the Chalet School, but installed at "Die Rosen" on the marriage of her adored mistress. Marie was now the wife of the doctor's man, Andreas, and mother, herself, of a two-month-old daughter. Whilst she cleared the china away, they talked idly about various subjects.

"What a house this is for babies!" said Joyce suddenly when Marie had gone.

"It is, rather," agreed Jo. "And when my sister-in-law

comes home in the summer as she thinks of doing, there'll be two more."

"Two!" said Cornelia. "I thought there was only Bridget?"

"So there was. But Mollie had another baby at Christmas—a boy, so they've called him John Noel, to be known as Jack. Didn't you hear? I thought I'd told everyone."

"Never heard a word of it," said Cornelia. Then she added, "I wonder what name they'll choose for the baby really?"

"I've no idea," said Joey. "I can tell you one thing, though. I'm certain it won't be either Esmeralda or Otillie! —As for you, Ruth, what have you been reading lately? I'm sure you never heard the name Esmeralda out of a book."

"Well, it *was* in a book," admitted Ruth, "but I thought it was a lovely name, and *so* uncommon."

"Uncommon all right. Rather too much so, in my estimation."

"You could always shorten it to Esme, I suppose," said Cornelia. "But I bar toshy names like that all the time. Give me a good plain handle."

"Yes; what's wrong with your own name that you've taken such a dislike to fancy ones?" demanded Jo, suddenly sitting erect. "Cornelia isn't as bad as all that comes to."

Cornelia was in an expansive mood, and she now let slip the secret she had carefully preserved all her school-life. "It isn't only that. I don't mind that so much myself. It's the rest that's such a mess-up."

"The rest? I never knew you had any more. All your things are marked 'C.F.' What else is there?" asked Joyce.

"That's because I made Poppa agree to it. Momma chose the rest, and he always hated it, so he didn't mind," explained Cornelia, whose mother had died when she was a few months old, so that she had no feeling for her, most of her life having been spent at once school or another.

"Well, what is it?"

"Swear you'll tell nobody?" said Cornelia cautiously.

"Of course we will. Go on, Corney. It can't be so awful as all that!"

"Guess it's the worst ever. I'm Cornelia Naida Anastasia Flower. Can you beat it?" said Cornelia with a deep sigh.

"Whew!" whistled Jo. "What a signature for a cheque! You're right, Corney. I'm not surprised you've sat on it all this time. I'd sit on a thing like that myself. Thank goodness, I'm plain Josephine Mary!"

However, when they were back at school again, they heard, to their vast indignation, that their labours of that afternoon had been in vain. Dr. Jem, now at a safe distance from reprisals, calmly wrote to his sister-in-law that Madge had laughed till she nearly cried over the list, and then had refused to have anything to do with any of them. The baby was to be Sybil Margaret, Sybil being her own favourite name.

"So all our work went for nothing," said the disgusted Jo. "I believe it was a put-up job on Jem's part. Well, it's the last time I'll ever bother my head to choose a name for a kid—that's certain!"

"Oh, but you will have to choose for your own," said Marie von Eschenau, who, now that she was almost eighteen, was beginning to think seriously about such things.

"Don't mean to have any—don't mean to marry," said Jo.

Marie laughed. "You may not now. But you do not know what the future may bring."

"I'm going to be an authoress. I'll have enough to do finding names for my characters and bringing them safely through all their woes and trials without setting up a family on my own. Besides, every nice family should have a charming maiden aunt. I'm going to be the one in ours. What with the Robin and David and Sybil, to say nothing of the twins and Bridget and Jack, my work will be cut out for me."

"You may say so now," said Marie, "but time will show all things."

"Oh, for goodness' sake don't talks in truisms! Be original, my child, whatever else you are. And *if* I ever do marry—and it's only *if*, remember—it won't be until I'm an aged dame, and wanting someone to trot me round in a bath-chair."

With which appalling sentiment, Jo declared the discussion closed, and went off to seek Joyce and Cornelia, and tell them what the baby's name finally was to be.

Have you read the adventures in the "Mystery" series by Enid Blyton?

THE ROCKINGDOWN MYSTERY

Staying at Rockingdown Hall, Roger, Diana, Snubby and Barney hear strange noises in the cellars. Barney goes to investigate and makes a very startling discovery . . .

THE RILLOBY FAIR MYSTERY

Valuable papers have disappeared – the Green Hands Gang has struck again! Which of Barney's workmates at the circus is responsible? The four friends turn detectives – and have to tackle a dangerous criminal.

THE RUBADUB MYSTERY

Who is the enemy agent at the top-secret submarine harbour? Roger, Diana, Snubby and Barney are determined to find out – and find themselves in a most exciting mystery.

THE RING O'BELLS MYSTERY

Eerie events have been happening at deserted Ring O'Bells Hall – and they spark off another mystery for the four friends to solve.

THE RAT-A-TAT MYSTERY

When the big knocker on the ancient door of Rat-a-tat House bangs by itself in the middle of the night, it heralds a series of very peculiar happenings – and another action-packed adventure for Roger, Diana, Snubby and Barney.

THE RAGAMUFFIN MYSTERY

"This is going to be the most exciting holiday we've ever had," said Roger – and little does he know how true his words will prove when he and his three friends go to Merlin's Cove and discover the hideout of a gang of thieves.

Armada

MILL GREEN

School Series

by Alison Prince

Now there's a great new school series in Armada.

Mill Green is a big, new comprehensive – with more than its fair share of dramas and disasters! Get to know Matt, Danny, Rachel, and the rest of the First Form mob in their first two exciting adventures.

Mill Green on Fire
When someone starts fires in the school and blames the caretaker, Matt is determined to catch the real culprit. But his brilliant plan to catch the firebug goes horribly wrong . . .

Mill Green on Stage
The First Formers prepare for the Christmas pantomime – and sparks soon fly when Marcia Mudd, a ghastly new girl, gets the best part. But when Matt locks Marcia in a cupboard and she disappears from the school, there's big trouble for everyone . . .

More stories about Mill Green will be published in Armada.

Armada

HI KIDS!
I'VE GOT THE
POWER TO BRING YOU FUN,
ADVENTURE, AND
EXCITEMENT!

Here are just some of the best-selling
titles that Armada has to offer:

☐ **The Whizzkid's Handbook 2** Peter Eldin 95p

☐ **The Vanishing Thieves** Franklin W. Dixon 95p

☐ **14th Armada Ghost Book** Mary Danby 85p

☐ **The Chalet School and Richenda** Elinor M. Brent-Dyer 95p

☐ **The Even More Awful Joke Book** Mary Danby 95p

☐ **Adventure Stories** Enid Blyton 85p

☐ **Biggles Learns to Fly** Captain W. E. Johns 90p

☐ **The Mystery of Horseshoe Canyon** Ann Sheldon 95p

☐ **Mill Green on Stage** Alison Prince 95p

☐ **The Mystery of the Sinister Scarecrow** Alfred Hitchcock 95p

☐ **The Secret of Shadow Ranch** Carolyn Keene 95p

Armadas are available in bookshops and newsagents, but can also be
ordered by post.

HOW TO ORDER
ARMADA BOOKS, Cash Sales Dept., GPO Box 29, Douglas, Isle of
Man, British Isles. Please send purchase price of book plus postage,
as follows:–

    1–4 Books .... 10p per copy
    5 Books or more . . . . no further charge
    25 Books sent post free within U.K.

Overseas Customers: 12p per copy

NAME (Block letters)

ADDRESS